BLACK VELLUM

Ansgar Allen

SCHISM²

First published in 2023 by Schism 2

First edition
ISBN: 9781739770891

Cover detail from 'The Vigilant Eye' by Jacques Callot 1628

FIELD NOTES

Scope of Field Notes.—The notes should be a complete record of each day's work in the field. In addition to the title of the problem and the record of the data observed, the field notes should include the date, weather, organization of party, equipment used, time devoted to the problem and any other information which is at all likely to be of service in connection with the problem. No item properly belonging to the notes should be trusted to memory. Should the question arise as to the desirability of any item, it is always safe to include it. The habit of rigid self-criticism of the field notes should be cultivated.

Character of Notes.—The field notes should have character and force. As a rule, the general character of the student's work can be judged with considerable certainty by the appearance of his field notes. A first-class page of field notes always commands respect, and tends to establish and stimulate confidence in the recorder. The notes should be arranged systematically.

Interpretation of Notes.—The field notes should have one and only one reasonable interpretation, and that the correct one. They should be perfectly legible and easily understood by anyone at all familiar with such matters.

Original Notes.—Each student must keep complete notes of each problem. Field notes must not be taken on loose slips or sheets of paper or in other notebooks, but the *original record* must be put in the prescribed field notebook *during the progress of the field work*.

Field Notebook.—The field record must be kept in the prescribed field notebook. For ease of identification the name of the owner will be printed in bold letters at the top of the front cover of the field notebook.

Pencil.—To insure permanency all notes will be kept with a hard pencil, preferably a 4H. The pencil should be kept well sharpened and used with sufficient pressure to indent the surface of the paper somewhat.

Title Page.—An appropriate title page will be printed on the first page of the field notebook.

Indexing and Cross-referencing.—A systematic index of the field notes will be kept on the four pages following the title page. Related notes on different pages will be liberally and plainly cross-referenced. The pages of the notebook will be numbered to facilitate indexing.

Methods of Recording Field Notes.—There are three general methods of recording field notes, namely: (1) by sketch, (2) by description or narration, and (3) by tabulation. It is not uncommon to combine two or perhaps all three of these methods in the same problem or survey.

Form of Notes.—All field notes must be recorded in a field notebook ruled as shown below, except where circumstances require modification. If no form is given, the student will devise one suited to the particular problem.

Lettering.—Field notes will be printed habitually in the *Engineering News* style of free-hand lettering, as treated in Reinhardt's "Freehand Lettering." The body of the field notes will be recorded in the slanting

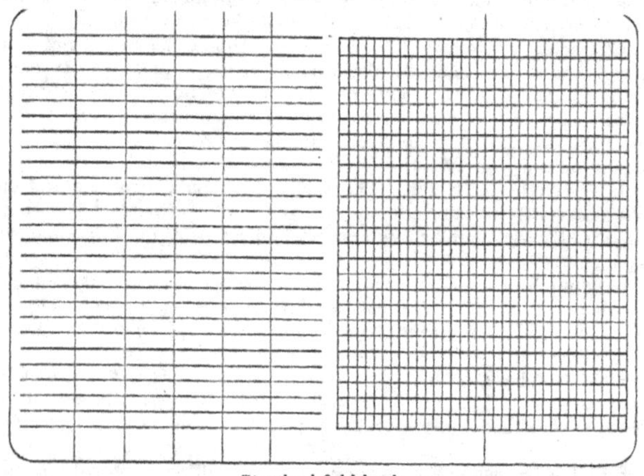

Standard field book.

letter and the headings will be made in the upright letter. The former slants to the right 1:2.5, and the so-called upright letter is made to slant to the left slightly, say 1:25. Lower case letters will be used in general, capitals being employed for initials and important words, as required. In the standard field note alphabet the height of lower case letters a, c, e, i, m, n, etc., is $\frac{3}{40}$ inch, and the height of lower case b, d, f, g, h, etc., and of all capital letters and all numerals is $\frac{5}{40}$ ($\frac{1}{8}$) inch; lower case t is made four units ($\frac{4}{40}$) inch high. This standard accords with best current practice and is based upon correct economic principles. Sample pages of field notes with letters and figures drawn full size are given on page 9. The student is expected to make the most of this opportunity to secure a liberal amount of practice in free-hand lettering.

Field-note Sketches.—Sketches will be used liberally in the notes and will be made *in the field.* If desired, a ruler may be used in drawing straight lines, but the student is urged to acquire skill at once in making good plain free-hand sketches. The field sketches should be bold and clear, in fair proportion and of liberal size so as to avoid confusion of detail. The exaggeration of certain details in a separate sketch sometimes adds greatly to the clearness of the notes. The sketches should be supplemented by descriptive statements when helpful, and important points of the sketch should be lettered for reference. The precise scaling of sketches in the field notebook, while sometimes necessary, is usually undesirable owing to the time consumed. It is also found that undue attention to the drafting of the sketch is very apt to occupy the mind and cause omissions of important numerical data. Since recorded figures, and not the size of the field sketch itself, must usually be employed in the subsequent use of the notes, it is important to review the record *before leaving the field* to detect omissions or inconsistencies. Making sketches on loose sheets or in other books and subsequently copying them into the regular field book is very objectionable practice and will not be permitted in the class work. ·Copies of field notes or sketches are never as trustworthy as the original record made *during the progress* of the field work. In very rapid surveys where legibility of the original record must perhaps suffer somewhat, it is excellent practice to transcribe the notes at once to a neighboring page, thus preserving the original rough notes for future reference. The original has more weight as evidence, but the neat copy made before the notes are cold is of great help in interpreting them.

Numerical Data.—The record of numerical data should be consistent with the precision of the survey. In observations of the same class a uniform number of decimal places should be recorded. When the fraction in a result is exactly one-half the smallest unit or decimal place to be observed, record the even unit. Careful attention should be given to the *legibility of numerals.* This is a matter in which the beginner is often very weak. This defect can be corrected best by giving studious attention and practice to both the form and the vertical alinement of tabulated numerals.

Erasures.—Erasures in the field notes should be avoided. In case a figure is incorrectly recorded, it should be crossed out and the correct entry made near by. The neat cancellation of an item in the notes inspires confidence, but evidence of an erasure or alteration casts doubt

LENGTH OF THE METRE.

In a book published by the Ordnance Survey, entitled, "Comparison of Standards of Length," by Captain A. R. Clarke, R.E., F.R.S., 1866, will be found an elaborate account of the methods employed to determine the values of the principal national units of length in terms of each other. The most important relation is the following :—

$$\text{THE METRE} = 1\cdot093623 \text{ yard.}$$
$$= 39\cdot37043 \text{ inches.}$$

$$\text{THE YARD} = 0\cdot914392 \text{ metre.}$$

A quick test of the assertion that enjoyment outweighs pain in this world, or that they are at any rate balanced, would be to compare the feelings of an animal engaged in eating another with those of the animal being eaten.

Arthur Schopenhauer

The rock on which he sat. The tree. These last rays of light. No life consists of moments like this, he wrote, no human life at least. Nothing that a human calls or thinks of as life may be constructed from experiences of this sort. Those elements would not articulate with one another, learn to breathe, cough, and finally curse the mess which some, improbably, still call humanity. He left the conventions of his living being there, like this, and saw his living mocked by the bluntness of these objects. His was paused because he felt his thinking, which meant he also sensed its absence. He saw his surroundings with the workings of a mind let into its wake, temporarily released of its thoughts, its recollections, and its troubles. His own was held before itself, within a moment which was driven by nothing beyond itself. I have dwelled too long already by looking at them like this, he wrote. The rock. The tree. The light.

As I write these notes on this rock I am called back away by my habits. My perception of them was nothing like I would ordinarily see them. I have long seen things with a land surveyor's gaze, as they called it then. I have come to see myself seeing that way, in the manner they described, parsing each rock and each tree into segments of time or features of a landscape to be, over it, built—the tree razed, the rock hauled off—if I would see them at all. They said I no longer saw objects, merely the land underneath. You have become fixated on the contours, they would tell me next, and even these curves your eyes will cut through. Everything else is already gone from the surface of this earth and there is a trench along your line of sight. My land surveyor's perception—the first act of destruction. With your surveyor's perception, you have already destroyed the world. When I was taught to see with these eyes, I was torn from everything they told me about the inertias of our planet and its indifferences.

We are made of large, intervening periods of habitual movement, I read, or barely conscious living, misremembered as intentional acts. These vast slabs of time divide out those glimpses of a world unfreighted by the preoccupations of moving from one thing to another. Human living is dependent on their forgetting, he wrote, presumably still sitting on his rock. Moments like these must be forgotten and the forgetting of them must be forgotten too or their forgetting would be unbearable. This moment by the tree punctures my experience of moving onwards, it does not constitute my outlook, he went on. The sun to warm the side of his face and a pipe to smoke with. All of which signalled a feeling nearing satisfaction, close to oblivion, and was noted down as such and so taken forward and away from the time when he sat on a small rock next to a tree, eyes wrinkled in the face of it. His recollection of being there and of his musings, which were proof of his not being there, in their way, was all of it recorded in the book as a memory of a feeling once had, overlaid, necessarily, by his recalling and rebuilding of the thoughts which intruded upon it and signalled its unreachable extent. The smoke dissipated and accumulated. The bowl warmed his palm. It was too hot he always smoked it too hot. As he tapped the ash he thought he was doing that wrong too. He should not tap the pipe upturned against the rim but find a twig as he usually did when he remembered not to tap, and use the twig to gouge it out. He wrote it down in an attempt to make the overall effect mean something more than it was. I smoked it too hot again. I always smoke my pipe with too much enthusiasm or is it haste. Either way the bowl is over-heated. He watched two horseflies on the bark cleaning their heads—now surely dust—until his bowels motioned and the urgency of moving on set in. Together with the stiffness of his legs, arranged crossed over and cutting circulation to his shins, this sense of the need to make on announced the final ruin of his pleasure, or of the time it had taken for him to realise this setting, swiftly receding, had seen its arrival. The muck and fever of human living was hardly redeemed by the short pause he took to notice his surrounds and then see himself as a feature of them. He sat, and looked, and smoked, as if regarding it all from the outside, auditing his own outlook before itself. The fly which landed on his finger, and bit at it, was not thought about until it was gone, after which he inspected closely at where he supposed the fly had sunk its jaws, or its mandible parts, and communicated pain to the joint. He looked at the lowest hinge of his finger, there reddened, and felt the pain develop, and thought the fly must have landed when his hand was still propped against the rock to keep him seated.

That was written in precarious script against segments of illegible shorthand. There were diagrams. These occurred later in the book. Land surveyor's diagrams, rough sketches for reproducing in pen and ink—as surveyors do. These initial diagrams functioned as memory aides; they conveyed the information necessary for precision drawing. As with his handwriting, these sketches were marked with a tremor, although they did not so closely approach, as his written hand did, the frantic lines of what one day would be called the seismograph—or the Earthquake Machine, as James Lind called his—as if the spool had been run, and re-run, inking over its readings to produce an overlay, sensitive, layered, and ultimately indecipherable.

All introspection was set to falsify this event with retrospection. He wrote that too. It would falsify the moment with a memory of first entering this valley. His introspections would also falsify the event with projections as well, mostly the force of his anticipations. He thought of the rift, of this valley which went along and down its coursing and meandering to where he was told they hauled at the boulder. Anticipation of the boulder intruded upon the moment when he sat in the sun, and it coloured his experience of the light. Thought of which, and his assignment to measure its particulars, and motions—there had been reports of movement—intruded on his experience of the minor rock and the tree.

This was how the author described it or rendered something of the sort in the notebook given me some time ago, wrapped in black vellum, and which I have only just started to read.

There was a further note—. Somebody once said, chief among the satisfactions of smoking is how the activity expends time to no purpose. A smoker achieves temporary detachment from the demands of human industry. In my case, I believe, this holds to be true. I do not smoke too fast to be done with the doing of smoking, so I think, but from too much initial puffing—I used to call it my exuberance, but I am growing old for the word, it no longer applies— puffing then to light it, and perhaps the impatience of a fatigued mind wishing to be done with thinking.

This note was accompanied by several further reflections spaced out, one can suppose, by intervals of walking.

—That person also wrote, a foul stench marks the presence of life and we had better get used to it. I never took this as a rejection of life as such, but as an objection to those who claim not to smell it, or who think or write as if they had no idea. But I, for my part, have measured over so many dung heaps and fallen backwards into enough latrines and drains during the course of my surveys not to forget the stench. Although the smell of the living is emitted by the other orifices too. Most probably that author had all human activity in mind, and not merely the obvious, in writing about life being accompanied by a bad odour. The breath of a freshly woken child, for instance.

—If one of the chief satisfactions of smoking is how it squanders time and conjures absence, true smokers must indulge their habit asocially, or smoke only with those who do not speak and do not threaten to speak. It suits me to think this, I suppose, since I tend to smoke most when escaping work, and when alone.

—But that same somebody wrote too that this condition, or something like it—this condition of the experience of something that could be imagined, almost, to be a presentiment of oblivion—is the only basis of communication.

—And that the best communicators are those who do not press too hard on others, but are prepared to let things slide, and yield to that silence.

—About all counts I am not well decided. But it is clear to me that smoking is primarily wasteful. Smoking makes no claims to industry. When I smoke, I cannot work— not if I smoke properly—and I cannot write, not really, not without betraying the passivity of smoking to the demands of activity. I think some kinds of writing might aim for this oblivion too, the land surveyor wrote. Writing never written to be read is the obvious example—texts destroyed as soon as they are done. These texts are primarily wasteful, having intended no future, and succeeding in that intention to the extent they are destroyed, or lost, overlooked, or forgotten. But there are texts written to be read which might be considered in this way too. Texts which are not destroyed but can be thought of, still, in terms of their primary wastefulness. These encourage the reader to wonder repeatedly if they were wrong to begin reading, still wrong to continue reading, and yet—and this is crucial—draw the reader on and into their desolation.

At the place of the rock on which he perched, and on which he was prompted to these introspections, the rift valley was only a gentle incursion into the earth, a murmur of its possibilities, the fold inward and down still gradual and not all that much in depth. The upper edges of the rim felt reachable with an outstretched arm. The flatness of the land beyond those edges was attainable. The tree alongside was shaped by the wind which came over the horizon. This wind from the flat was only diminished in force as the woods thickened and the valley cut increased and receded into the crust of the planet. The gradients at this point were not worth measuring. The rift valley was unremarkable at its upper reaches and might be taken for what it was not, an ordinary depression. But those gentle lines in the earth and their overall effect did not escape his notice as he stood again and gathered his bags and equipment, the ranging rods, levelling staff, the tripod and its theodolite. His assistant stood too and was persuaded to take the rods by placing them in his arms, and so they proceeded. He gave the rods and the two of them commenced, the second behind the first, walking further down the valley into its coming fissure.

I put the lot down—his notebook and the vellum—so to peel the calf skin away from where it stuck to my fingers. When the notebook was given with a nod, the vellum was dripping, and the book inside sodden at the edges. It was in no condition to be read. And still now the vellum is moist, which is inexplicable seeing where I stored it and the length of time I left it to dry out. The notebook paper has become crisp, as wet pages dried hold their shape with greater resolution than before they were wetted. Only the vellum is damp, its ability to retain water exceeded in its deterioration. Vellum should not decay like this, I thought, and what material can hold water so long and under such conditions as I had created.

Further down the valley he came across the first ropemakers—. We stood and patiently regarded them, waiting for a pause in their activity. There was a low mist. It was the dust of their movement and the materials they worked with. Two men were beating bunches of hemp to extract fibres from the carcass. The first beating was done within a raised and hollowed trunk in which the hemp was trapped with heavy blows from a hinged bludgeon and then tugged through. After that the fibres resembling a horse tail I thought were held over a post and beaten with a flat pallet. This deprived the bundle of its coarseness and transformed it into a mop of blond hair. After so much beating each bundle of fibres was drawn through a rake of long nails, so he wrote, thrown over that rake and repeatedly pulled and then gathered and tied once the shortest fibres had been taken out and discarded. They did not look up as we came closer, and so we eventually sat very near and watched them at their work, beating and drawing and wrapping up bundles of hemp fibre ready to be spun into the first threads. At the loom one man turned the handle whilst the other walked backwards, spinning from the bundle he now wore as a girdle. He fed its fibres from the waist and to his fist and out through a wet rag. The rag was held in the palm and trapped between fingers which functioned as a gauge. Gradually his girdle diminished as fibres were spun out. These narrow strings were then wound into the first cords by the spinning wheel, each hung off its hooks, and by walking backwards with a rutted block of wood along and within the lines. The finished cords were laid over trusses, each cord arranged between vertical treenails, after which the two men drew their hands along the lines, one man after the other, leaning in, holding a wetted mesh in the fist, scouring, exfoliating the cords of their roughness and so their impurities. The two ropemakers were entirely consumed by their activity—the correct tension, sufficient incorporation of fibre, the right rate of turning, the harshness of their scouring, and then the drying that was done by a similar action. We left them at it and descended further into the valley, through the trees which grew thickly there, and down the slopes and banks.

My aim and principle—to stay in the vicinity of the river in its travel downwards. Both for its water and its orientation. This river eludes us repeatedly. And then we fall upon it.

From the vantage of my descent, he wrote, the complex struck me as an extension of the earth, a kind of levelling-out, a large clearing in the woods of the sort which must have existed (but how?) in the primal forests of our ancestors. The downward fall of the bank merely banked off as can happen to form a gently corrugated expanse of low vegetation. Viewed from above it was solid ground, and if not natural, it was surely an ancient formation, resolidified and returned to the crust. This may have been a foundation of some kind, earthworks perhaps, long abandoned and gently grown over. There was nothing to indicate, so I told myself later, nothing to tell this was in actuality the upper part of a still-living community industriously at work below my feet. Anyone else, descending as we did, and from the particular angle we took, would have seen it as I saw it, surely enough they would have seen it that way. I reached the terrace and began to walk across its surface, still thinking it to be earth, spongy and yielding, but this was due to the moss. It was a reasonable effect of the vegetation and not yet an argument against my assumption. My realisation that it was entirely artificial, and that the land beneath my feet was elevated on stilts or props, or beams and posts, came to me as a mild but definite sensation of vertiginous horror. The security of presumed earth fell away to the growing suspicion of something far less substantial, the knowledge that it was hollow below and this, here, was mere suspended surface. To a land surveyor of all people, it arrived as a particularly shocking if not painfully embarrassing awareness. I think I did my best to conceal my surprise and remain composed as my assistant caught me up. He was again carrying the rods I had once more encouraged him to hold by picking them up, and placing them in his arms. He stopped as I halted, still holding the rods, although he would surely drop them soon, I thought. Any time now he will drop the rods, I told myself. He will drop them here, only now they will not fall to the earth, but to this insubstantial skin. It was the sound of creaking which alerted me to the activity below. I crouched down to listen more closely and hear the draw of it, the series of groans which are made by slowly tightening rope. I fancied I could hear them treading up and down the rope walk, and that I could all but see them exfoliating the cords they made, just as we had seen them do further up the valley. It was the same rasping sound, I thought, but as I listened again, I could hear it was my own breath. My fists were tight, and the leather I wore creaked like the rope I had heard. There was still good enough reason to persuade myself against my suspicions. But I pushed my finger into the moss, and then my hand, and forced through to the thatch. It was unmistakable. The straw was bunched together and packed tightly, held in place by spars. We are standing on a roof, I told him, pointing at the bare patch of rotting thatch I had excavated. I indicated the terrain about us with a more expansive gesture, and said, these are roofs, but my assistant only answered my discovery by resuming his monologue. I pointed to each roof and told him these were huts, all huts, and that each hut by its narrowness and its length must surely contain a rope walk, and he continued to tell me about what he did before he was employed as my assistant. This terrace, I was now realising, was entirely formed of buildings arranged in parallel and grown over. The pitch of each roof was shallow, and the vegetation in the lower parts taller, reducing and softening the undulating profile. There were small gaps between each hut which I discovered by crawling there and extending my arm into the long crevice. Vegetation had stretched across the eaves so the languid covering of moss formed a continuous and slow-growing carpet raised at points by small grasses and other feeble plants, all of it shaded by the surrounding woodland. Following me as I crawled to the eaves and as I confronted my suspicion by reaching downward into the cavity, he came to stand very close to the concealed gap, ignored my descriptions, and so too my warnings, and went on with his monologue about what he had done before he worked for me, although he had never actually worked for me, I thought, not properly. As far as I was concerned, he exhausted his usefulness the moment he passed into my employment, that is, as soon as we entered the valley. The man was only formally engaged when I first employed him. Nothing he did exceeded that formality, or even realised it.

He accepted his contract, this was true, and continued to indicate as much by following me, as he did, but my assistant had never honoured the agreement, not really. I found him at the rift valley top newly released from his former employer and invited him to join me, and no sooner had I done so, he became useless to me. As we began our descent into the valley it became apparent my assistant was a poor choice. If he was not entirely functionless, he was very nearly so. I had given him the rods, and sometimes the staff and the tripod to carry, but not the theodolite, which is delicate, and he held them for a while, and he walked with them for some steps, but was soon distracted by the account of his former employment. He took that up by no means at its beginning. This was my feeling upon first hearing it. He did not introduce me to this story of his, nor prepare me in any way for it. There were no preparational words. He did not establish the grounds of his telling or gain my consent as his listener. It merely took up as if he were already telling in his head. To the extent I listened— and at first, I hardly did—I was required to piece it together, gathering details, working against those that were assumed, or perhaps told before we first met. His narrative suffered too from what seemed to me definite absences or gaps, cuts in temporality. At other times he halted as if searching for a word, resuming again as if there had been no gap. But it was also enormously detailed, and suggested a prodigious skill at recollection, or at least a high skill at improvisation. In telling his account I too must improvise (I am forced to), but feel I have rendered his words accurately, or well enough. At times he would put the equipment down on the ground or lean it against a tree so he could better gesticulate with the telling of his former employment, and I, for my part, took to lifting the equipment and placing it back in his arms as the easiest means of resuming our journey together. There was no interrupting nor asking him to pick them up. The rods could only be placed into his stomach horizontally, whereupon his arms rose by reflex, hands cupped round. By the time we reached the terrace I was accustomed to it, returning the rods to his grasp almost without thinking each time he dropped them. He was not permanently in this state of discourse, or telling, which was fortunate, and this made his presence bearable, although the impossibility of dismissing him given our mutual entrapment in the valley was still painful to me even during these silences. His contemplative moods were not in truth breaks from his telling but weighed at me with the threat of further talk. This meant all his silences were overdetermined by the surety of resumption, now propelled with the built-up inertia gained during the absence of his talking. Crawling back to the apex of this particular hut, I sat down to make a record of my discovery. Seeing me unwrap my notebook my assistant indicated towards the vellum, or vellum-like material I use to that purpose, and said, *we had something like that for his pupils.* I looked up and saw him point at the vellum, or this material which resembles black vellum, as I folded it away and placed it in my bag. That caused him to bend over at the knees and from the waist, oddly twisted to the side. He did this so he could still see the edges of the wrapping within my bag, and thereby continue to point and strike the black sheet with his imaginary line and say again, *that is what we used.* Exactly that is what we used, he assured me—still pointing—we used something like that, he said, as I opened my notebook and prepared to write whatever it was I intended to be writing at that point. He did not remark upon my activity or react in any way to my frequent pauses to keep record, nor did he ever ask what I was setting down. He often stood close enough to see the page, but I was sure he could not decipher the shorthand which I would, each evening, work to transcribe and fill out. It is my own invention, or at least, this shorthand is sufficiently adapted to be illegible to anyone but me. Neither did he ask about the figures I entered to record our altitude at the end of each entry—we were still above sea level at this point—nor did he remark on anything else I did, or what we were doing, or where we were going. When I first employed him, he did not ask me anything, such as to furnish him with any particulars beyond the bare description I gave—*I need your help in carrying my equipment, please, my mule is dead.* He did not even say yes, or, yes I will accompany you, or, for how long, or, what is our destination, or even, what happened to the mule. I was stood by the mule when he came walking down the track. The mule was lying there at my feet, its mouth gaping, its eyes too, but he did not comment upon the mule when presented with it. I beckoned him over. Without my doing that, without my calling and my waving, he would not have come. I suspect he was about to walk straight past. Not from decision. There was nothing deliberate about his not looking at me when he first came down that path. As he approached, I could see he was not seeing me in a purely accidental way. He came into the clearing in which the mule lay and I stood, and he did not lift his eye gaze in our direction at all. It was clear to me he was making no deliberate effort to not see us. He is not trying to not see me, I thought, he just happens to be not looking, which is entirely different. It is easy to tell between the two. When somebody is not looking because they have decided against it, this not looking is as good as looking. I have quite deliberately not looked at people myself and have always felt in doing so, in my decisive not looking, that I am effectively looking at them and that they can probably tell. When not looking at someone, the eyes, which should be looking elsewhere, are actually now unseeing eyes because they are focused on the activity of not seeing. Not looking at someone even when facing in the other direction takes conscious effort. And so I had to shout, look here, I shouted, not resenting him for not yet looking despite the miserable arrangement of the mule at my feet. Look here, I said, I really am in a fix. This mule is lying on my equipment. He came over and I told him to help me lift so we could pull the saddle bag out on the other side, which he did, which we both did, hauling with good effort, kicking the saddle bag out with my feet as the mule was lifted a fraction, and with me then saying something more about the mule, about it dying, and about the way it collapsed, and how my equipment became trapped. And as I said it all, still he did not comment on my predicament or really acknowledge what I had to say. He seemed indifferent to it, as if the entire scene did not properly register in his consciousness. Which meant from the moment I employed him he was indifferently employed. As soon as he came into my command—which he did by following me, as I told him to, and which following I took to be an agreement—his chief and only concern was the activity of recollection. He did now see me—I saw this clearly—and he heard me too, but what he saw and what he heard remained at the edges of his seeing and his hearing. Looking at where I had stowed the vellum he said, *we cut little circles out of the material with a knife.* He told me this as I crouched by the apex, pencil in hand. And these circles we laid at the centre of each eyeball, he went on. We took the eyeball, held it between the fingers of one hand, and with the other grasped the little piece of black material, the cut-out, the small circle, which we had laid on another, larger circle, grey, cut from mottled paper, and stuck all of it together on the white of the egg with a little spittle. This fixed it well enough until we applied a thin coat of glaze. The glaze we made from boiling calves' feet, mostly, or some other substitute, I cannot remember. Can I remember, no I cannot, he said. In any case, these little black circles produced the effect of dilated pupils once they were stuck and glazed. With the eyes inserted into their sockets, our black circles looked outwards and, so they say, peered into the soul. Every time we cut them and stuck them with our spittle, the pupils were dilated, or so it seemed to us. They were larger than they should be, we thought. This was not deliberate, he said, we cut them as smoothly and tightly as we could. But the eyes we produced were always dilated eyes. If we cut them smaller we could not cut them round. The pupils we made when we cut them small were angular ovals with sharp turns from the instruments we used. This gave them a deformed aspect when placed on the eye and the eye was entirely useless in the work of peering, he said, or at least, in the work of being peered at, because it was clearly a false eye poorly made—an eye with corners. And so it was resolved we would produce dilated pupils as the best approximation. These dilated pupils were nonetheless perfect, we thought, and holding the eggs in our hands we very nearly convinced ourselves we held eyes.

Listening to this I finished my report, folded my notebook back into the black vellum, and stood up, wondering how we might get down from the terrace and to the entrances below. These pupils, he said, did the job well enough. I improvise, necessarily, but that is the gist of what he next told me. They might even be considered an improvement, he continued, a better approximation of the priest's eyes, since we modelled them on the priest when the priest was stood before us, his pupils shrunken to black points. In the harsh light that was necessary for our work, his eyes were constricted fists, staring with the harshness of extreme myosis. This was our mistake. When we studied his gaze, we studied it wrongly. Having stared at his pupils and observed them closely, seeking as we did not merely to remake their shape, their colour, but re-engender the feeling of his looking upon others, we looked at the wrong eyes, and sought to reproduce the wrong effect. We never approximated the priest in his natural setting but saw and studied him in the unnatural setting of the workshop. We asked the priest to move into the light and by doing that failed him. By the time it came to the eyes, we were accustomed to our decision. We had decided only the best light would do, and that this spot by the south window is where we would ask him to stop, and be still, we said, so we might observe him closely enough to remake the folds of his skin, the feeling of its proximity, its faint moistures, and its animate warmth. Most of all we worked to reproduce the sensation we had that the skin of the priest encased recesses of persuasion only centuries could give to borrow from, this inheritance trod across parishes from one blessed kingdom to the next and to its blessed enemies. Their reckonings were turned in on themselves within this casement, we felt, and further accounted for the moisture. They contributed to the priest's unfathomable interiority. We felt that the flesh of his face was stretched over so as to barely contain the great force of its inwardness, and that each remaining fold was another refusal of his religion to lay itself open. Stretching our own skins to mimic his, wishing to reproduce the exact effect, we also developed these eyeballs to place in each hollow. As we sought to remake his eyes as perfect replicas of his looking, it did not occur to us in our first attempts, and our first dissatisfactions, that the larger pupils we crafted were a far better representation of the effect of his gaze in the poor light of those houses and hovels to which we sent our automaton to do his work. With these eyes in place, our manufactured eyes, we found the automaton need often merely stare, and not even gesticulate, for the supplicants to feel affected.

I gave him the rods again and walked to the edge of the roof, studying the compacted earth before the huts and the faint light which crept over it from under the doors. My assistant continued to talk, and I listened, but as I did so my gaze kept to the ground below. The mud by each entrance was casting shadows even though its depressions were shortest where the ground was most trampled. From the edge of the roof I could smell the vapours of the oil lamps they used to light their work. I could hear or imagine hearing them below, walking backwards with the first yarns and strands along each rope walk, hooking them on the jack, turning its wheels, bending and straightening at the crank.

We replaced the eyeballs, he said, when the reek of each eye, a peeled quail's egg, began to stink out the rest of the automaton. Sometimes we would have several pupils ready cut, several versions of the iris too, and would have only to boil the egg, he told me, and prepare the glaze. I walked back across the rooftops to the bank, beckoning him to follow, and then cut up and round and across to the left, encircling the development until we could find a way down further on. The day was drawing to its close and we would soon need to make camp, the trees above reducing to their outlines.

They stood briefly by the huts and the land surveyor lent in, so he wrote, to better hear the sounds and confirm his suspicion they were winding rope inside. From this vantage the listening was clearer and not muffled as before by the thatch. But the sounds were still overlaid. It took time and concentration to separate them out. He claimed he could hear the wheels, the noise of the crank, the wooden teeth interlocking. That he could distinguish at a further distance because fainter, the activity of them beating hemp as the two ropemakers first encountered above had done— the unmistakable sound of the hollowed trunk raised at an angle and hinged by a treenail to another interior spar, the bludgeon, between which the mass of hemp was smashed and drawn. He wrote that he could separate out the sound of the flat pallet as it struck against the post, and the rough, rasping of each hemp carcass after the dull blow which preceded it. He claimed to hear the treenail in its joint and the handle of the pallet in its rough and calloused hand. And behind all the blows and tempests of their work, the shouts and outbursts—they often cried out to one another in some indeterminate tongue—he could even hear the rake of nails on which each carcass was flung and through which it was pulled. It was as if I could hear the fibres themselves tugging, he wrote, and tearing individually against the sound of the nails, each nail its own length and vibrating at its own natural frequency. These nails were longer and thinner and more closely packed than any other kind of nail can be driven. The sound of hemp thrown over and dragged through them was enough to rake the skin. This noise grew about him and developed its own physicality, dwarfing the buildings and trees. The land surveyor confessed this was at least in part embellishment, and it was all set to confusion by the noise of their lower speech and the sound of their tongues and the wetness of their mouths—he claimed to hear that too. It is tempting to interpret this account as one of specific vibrations and unmistakable knocks only retrospectively introduced to his memory, and never in fact heard in person. Once I was satisfied by the impression of it all—so he wrote—having confirmed the nature of these huts and their industry, I decided to wait until morning. We made camp, he reported, using the poles to construct a shelter, as travelling land surveyors are known to do. We had removed ourselves over a small rise, no longer visible to the huts or the track which gathered from their entrances and that descended further into the valley. Our fire was small. My assistant fell into meditating, and I ate the last of our dried meat.

I woke to his talk. The priest, he was saying, openly wondered why he first designed the automaton, and asked himself repeatedly if it was merely for relief from his duties rather than some greater experiment in the derangement of human affect and outlook. Because this is how it came to appear in retrospect, the priest said. He could see it now for what it was, he told us, his experiment in the makings of human consciousness. Perhaps he did it first out of need, but what he accomplished, his great accomplishment as he called it, made it hard to imagine how this sense of need had once been felt. When somebody has done something magnificent, the priest told us, it is difficult to see how it came about without invoking the divine. There comes a point, he went on, when nothing makes sense without invoking the divine. As an extraordinary priest who frequently did extraordinary things, he was perhaps forced to invoke the divine more than most, he conceded, so much so it had become a tiresome reflex. Looking back, he said, it seemed to him that he had again achieved something of the sort, and what he had achieved had clearly exceeded its origins and was unthinkable in their terms. It had transcended them, he added. Well not entirely, he clarified, but largely. What he had made was not entirely disconnected from those origins. Clearly it was still linked to them in some way. But so much about his creation had nothing to do with them, of this he was also sure. And if those origins were lowly, as perhaps they were, these origins could not account for what they originated and what they originated could not be explained in lowly terms. There was an element of boredom or laziness at work too, he admitted, but it was not, it could not be mere boredom or simple laziness which made him do what he did, he told us. He was frequently bored, and his laziness was a product of that boredom. But his achievement should not be traced back to his boredom, or his boredom-induced laziness, with each—his laziness, his boredom—functioning as its sole causes. This would be mistaken, he said. Undoubtedly, he did wish for relief from his duties, from the largely repetitive nature of his work, because nothing is so sure to repeat itself, he told us, than human suffering, and nothing is so sure to make itself felt than the need to assuage human suffering, or at least, the need to have that suffering assuaged. Suffering is assured, and the need to have it assuaged it is assured, and nothing could be more tiresome. The only thing about human beings which can be predicted with certainty, he said, is the fact of their suffering. Human beings are destined to suffer, and then, to make matters worse, when they reach toward anything in thought or outlook that is even remotely complex, they wish to make sense of their suffering and reduce their suffering, which in many cases means finding ways of passing suffering on to another or seeing another suffer to reduce one's own pain. It was all so lamentably, so easily, so definitely repeatable. But for all that, human suffering had never entirely bored him, he said, which is the same as declaring human suffering had never entirely sated him. He was never entirely bored and never entirely sated by the spectacle of human suffering, the priest told us, even if so much of human suffering is predictable and repetitive and assured and plentiful, and as a priest he was forced to see a good deal more of it than most people. He was destined to see, as one might say, more than his fill, even if suffering in such volume, of such higher than ordinary frequency, was not enough to fill him up entirely. Everyone, he told us, has the capacity to spectate just a little bit more suffering. The sight of suffering will always draw interest. He knew this by observing himself, finding himself still able to spectate, still drawn to watch, still able to raise his head, after so many years of having all kinds of human suffering thrust before him for the priest to see, because if anyone suffers, it is a given fact, a law if you like, that they will wish to take their suffering to the priest. At the sight of religion, or the trappings of religion, human sufferers turn themselves into suffering projectiles, he said, always targeted at the local priest. And he had long grown tired of being pelted by all these suffering human projectiles. Even if he was not entirely bored by their suffering, even if it had not sated him yet, he was grown tired of it, he said, and was in need of a break. He accepted his existence depended upon being pelted in this way, but a rest from it might be good. He realised, so he said, how his life as a priest relied upon the fact he would be besieged, but perhaps if it were only on Sundays, and not every day or any day a member of his congregation felt afflicted. The fact of being besieged defined his priestly outlook, he knew. It was the fact of being a priest to look out and see them coming, limping towards him. A priest is defined by the suffering he attracts. A priest would not be a priest if all sufferers did not turn in their moments of greatest need in his direction. This must be admitted. It was an inescapable fact of his profession. He admitted it. He declared it. He was willing to declare the fact and some accompanying notions too. It was not the fact alone, he said, because a fact on its own is nothing. Whenever a fact is offered, he said, ask for the fact which accompanies it, gives it propulsion, and makes it true. And in this case, he told us, the accompanying fact is worth asking for. He knew as a priest he must face this onslaught because of that accompanying fact, the companion notion, the idea, which is to say, the statement of principle by which human beings mark themselves off as distinct, namely, the fancy, the conviction, that it is surely lamentable for human beings to have to suffer so much. Human beings look at their own suffering and wonder at it, and say, it is lamentable we suffer so badly and so often. Perhaps it is lamentable we suffer at all. This is the accompanying fact, he repeated. The fact of being a priest and the fact of attracting so much suffering is based in the fact of people thinking they surely do not deserve to suffer so badly. This is what brings them flocking in, and this is what defines my mission as I reply, in one way or another, directly or by circumlocution, they do indeed deserve to suffer as they do, a lesson they would not need if they did not always insist on the opposite. I present them with the rightful truth, which is the foundation of their lament, the point from which their lament departs, from which it flees. I return them to the cold slab of rock and they know it to be true, because all they have done, all which has defined them, is their attempt to escape into the apparent refinement of their reflections and the fog of their complaints. I merely bring them back down, and hold them there, and tell them—because this is my teaching—how there is no escape on earth from the suffering they have experienced and will continue to experience until they can feel nothing else. Without their suffering, and without this conviction of theirs that it is unfortunate to suffer so, the priest would have no purpose in the world. He would have nothing to tell them. He would have nobody to tell that yes, actually, your suffering is deserved. So, yes, his existence as a priest depended on being besieged. His function rested upon their conviction that of all the animals human beings somehow deserved their suffering least of all and so needed to be told they deserved it most of all. And, yes, he was bored with being besieged, and with telling the lesson, but the priest still managed to find something to entertain himself with, some minor detail to perseverate on within each example of human pain which presented itself before him. He told the lesson to them, and the lesson itself bored him most of all, but every well of pain, every moaning supplicant, did carry a lurid facet, a unique spasm, an odd symptom, for him to wonder at.

The prototype—by far inferior to the device later used—lay decaying in a corner of the workshop. It was still dressed in its cowl and habit. The arms were set, flung outward and stiff within the sleeves. Somebody had drawn over its hood to hide the mask and prevent us seeing its further deterioration. The exposed parts came to resemble the kind of necrotic tissue sometimes found on living creatures. The local lord—a minor ruler, not without reach or influence—had heard of the first automaton and of its conveyance from one hovel to another. He heard about it from a discrete observer of such things who went about the lord's dominion gathering curiosities. This self-anointed informer, a professional the man said of himself, strutted with the prides of a self-employed man. I am a professional informer, the man said when he first came strutting in and introduced himself to the lord. He ingratiated himself to the lord much as he ingratiated himself to the unsuspecting and credulous by filling their ears with lies and praises. When the informer was abroad, he would tell his lies and his praises while all the time listening for some profitable bit of information, some intrigue, some betrayal, some salacious titbit, for the lord to later chew on and for which purpose (and the favour it would bring) the informer would gather and preserve and suitably embellish each parcel of news, taken as such back to the seat of his power. This time he returned to the lord with a story of priestly intrigue. He had seen it himself, so he said, or so the priest later came to understand. The informer told the lord that he was sitting inside one of the peasant houses with his better ear listening to the peasants. He was hoping to hear of something improper, something witnessed by those who are often treated by their superiors as if they do not themselves have eyes or ears to see or hear with. For this reason, he said, peasants and other lowly people are often privy to the best, least disguised examples of higher waywardness, if only the informer could wade through their speech, thick with its own idioms and dark insights which people such as he could scarcely fathom and would never fully appreciate. Listening, deciphering, suffering the obscurity of their talk and perception, the informer was already there in the house that was to be visited by the priest's creation, and sat during the entire visit undetected. I was already there, he told the lord, and sat during the entire visit without being noticed by the visitor. This latter fact, the fact of not being noticed, became less remarkable, of course, as the informer came to the nub of his story and the fact which accompanied it. As it turned out, he found it not at all hard to hide from the visitor. It was quite by chance, the informer said. I was waiting quite by chance as the priest's automaton arrived. With its arrival the informer first suffered the very same deception intended for the peasants. He, too, experienced its false projections of priestly authority and priestly consolation as if they came with the force of conviction, and he suffered those projections most convincingly, he said, just as he suffered them in church. He could testify to that, to its deception, and testified willingly. I willingly admit, he said to the lord, his employer, even I was deceived at this point. It was a most ingenious deception, he told the lord. Devilishly effective, a deception of the first order, he said, and he would have remained deceived, indeed, had he not followed the priestly figure out of the house, assured by this point he would not after all learn anything profitable from this particular household of peasants however long he listened. Had he not followed he could not have learnt what he came to tell. Only after following, he went on, did I find out this bit of news I have for you. If I had not been there, the lord's informer continued, I would never have known. But let me retreat back a little and tell you about the impression it gave in the house. I must describe the deception first, he said, before I tell you how I uncovered it. When the priest figure was in the house, it did not invite any kind of personal approach and none present addressed it directly, they all retreated as it came in. The little recesses and crevices around the entrance room filled themselves with peasant rumps, he added—thinking it would amuse the lord to describe the activity of their rear ends that way—and the peasant children, so it seemed, he continued, retreated into the cracks by the walls. They were very thin, he added. Peasants tend to produce very thin children as you may know. You have perhaps noticed yourself how thin their children are. These children are hard to pick out from their surroundings because of their thinness. It is easier to see their adults when faced with a peasant crowd and ignore the fact of their children entirely. But once you begin to notice them, and pay attention, you start to see their thin little children everywhere and wonder how exactly the peasant stock regenerates, as it so reliably does, given the thinness of its offspring, with these ones in the hovel I am telling you about so thin they easily slipped behind the adults into the smaller cracks of the room. With them all arranged this way—the adults in their recesses, the children wedged in the cracks—I think even I retreated a little too, he added. Even I found a place to step back to from which I like the rest of them waited and endured the silence. This silence seemed to be what was expected of us. Our visitor stilled the air, or at least the air about our visitor was stilled, oddly stilled. If there had been light enough to see those particles of floating dust by—you know, he said, that dust, the minor firmament which floats about inside homes—*even these atmospheric movements would have been stilled*, I suspect, the informer said, thinking it would impress the lord for him to think that. In any case, the priest figure left all assembled with the definite impression nothing more was to be said, and that we should not come closer, or address him, or elicit words of any kind. In this case all felt, and this was my feeling too, the informer said, we should allow the visitor to retreat unheeded into his travelling solitude. The donkey backed out of the house, the hooded figure riding it ducked at the lintel, and they let it go without following. Ordinarily peasants will go after the priest into the yard. It is typical for peasants to trail a priest just as you are trailed in the streets, he said to the lord, and some will even travel up the lane behind their priest. Peasants will not go behind a priest as far as they go behind you, but they will walk a good way. When you ride past a peasant house, they flow out of it, they very nearly fall from each doorway, these peasants, to see you. Something similar happens with the priest. Only it happens when the priest leaves. When the priest rides past a peasant house they beckon him in. They do not come out as they do for you. But when he leaves, they follow out after him, and so the effect is similar. As a priest leaves a house it is vented of its occupants. The priest comes first and then the peasantry and their dirt. I have seen peasants walk a few hundred yards alongside and after a retreating priest, the informer said, whereas they will follow you for a good thousand yards or more, he added. But these peasants did not even move towards the door. And that is highly unusual. You might say, he told the lord, it was the sight of the donkey moving backwards which halted them. As every peasant knows, donkeys are not for walking in that manner. A donkey may take a few steps, but only a few, and these steps are clumsily done. After these first steps it will turn about. It was uncanny to see this donkey manoeuvre so deftly into the doorway, exiting with its rear as if its end had an eye or more to look with. This probably struck those present in the room as it struck me, he said. We all found it strikingly odd. But this was not the reason why we were reluctant to follow. Curiosity may indeed have taken the entire household of peasants outside to watch the donkey manoeuvre into the yard. But when none followed, they failed to do so because of its mount. I did not know it then, but later realised it so, the informer said. As the priest later interpreted, interpolating his own filament as he told the story, the figure on the donkey trailed a well of heaviness, a sensation of the void at the core of its being, and so drove his audience soon enough to will its exit. They did not know what it was that just visited them, most likely thinking it to be the priest in a taciturn mood. They were entirely taken in by the deception, he thought, and yet, they sensed its void and wished it gone. The automated priest had done its work, the priest said. And perhaps had done it more efficiently than usual, seeing as his visit was not drawn out. As the informer recounted, it was a very brief visit indeed. But I did go out, the informer told the lord with pride, and it is just as well I did. Despite my reluctance I followed the thing as it retreated. I was myself also done with my visit. A peasant hovel, you should know, he told the lord, is filled with bad air. It is the kind of air that tastes as it smells. It fills the peasant head with its bad vapours and bad outlooks. I endure it, of course, for the purposes of acquiring news, but I would not recommend a stay in a peasant hovel to anyone but a peasant, he said, and to a peasant it takes no recommending. Peasant air can only be endured by someone who has already grown up in that atmosphere and has learned to live with it from the earliest age and so has already been dulled by it from birth. You, your lordship, should have no reason ever to enter one of these hovels from which I bring you news, but if you ever do, bring perfumes and smelling bottles, line your scarf with scent and hold it close about the mouth and nose. By the time I emerged, he said, driven out of the hovel despite my reluctance to spend any time longer in the vicinity of our visitor, I saw how the figure was already retreating on its mount up the track, drawn by another, also in a hood, some kind of servant. But the informer was now able to look, so he said, and see the figure in the light, and so it was the informer saw with unmistaken clarity that its mount was not so much ridden as burdened by a man-shaped load. As he watched the priest figure retreat, he finally saw that cloaked revenant in the full light of its awful rigidity, dead and unfeeling, gathering up against the unyielding sun, sensing not the warmth of its fires, but projecting outwards rigor mortis and the destiny of flesh. The observer told his story, the full length of it and more, with hands already poised to receive his due, the reward he was accustomed to getting. It was his habit to hold his palms upward and very nearly together. This was his signature posture, one could say, as the priest said, a gesture that both announced and concluded his regular betrayal of the confidences and privacies of others. He handed over his gossip and received his monies with the same movement. The informer clearly felt he was betraying me to the lord, the priest said. He believed he was handing me over. The informer reckoned I wished to conceal what I had done and that I would be deprived of my lie if he told the lord. All of which shows he could not account for my indifference. The informer had no conception of my indifference, the priest said, and could never conceive of it since he was wedded to the idea of betrayal. My indifference would explode that idea if he allowed it to, if he had the capacity to see that not everything can be betrayed because some things are unmoved. *This is the doing of our priest*, the informer said to the lord. There is no other possible conclusion. None but the priest could bring off this effect. After I left the peasants, I could not find the actual priest, the informer went on, he was not where I looked, but sure enough it was him who had done this. It is the priest who has made this thing which now visits your subjects. Our priest, he told the lord, has given up the worst of his duties to a contrived priest-resembling mechanism, a moving structure made of animal flesh. The priest has this mechanism carried upon a donkey and led by a slave from one peasant house to another. The entire contraption is ridden in through narrow doorways, and tilted over in so doing, whereupon it gives sacrament by a mechanical nod and performs other such rites, breathing as the donkey inhales, shifting as the donkey itself motions with its restlessness and occasionally drops dung to the continued awe and supplication of those visited. Only the darkest houses will do, of course. This priest-resembling mechanism will not stand inspection in brighter places. But the peasantry lives in semi-darkness, and so the priest machine can safely visit them. They move about below heavy beams, allowing only little windows to vent their homes, the least air permitted to communicate with the world outside. The priest's double roves widely among them and travels across your dominion unrestrained, he said, or restrained only by the stamina of its carrier and the endurance of the slave that holds and pulls at its halter.

Upon hearing of the machine, the local lord knew how it might be put to use, the priest said. He understood its possibilities, although it should be pointed out, the priest added, that the lord's understanding remained of a very rudimentary sort. The lord saw with the clarity of his simplicity what the machine could achieve in the orbit of his dominion. The lord saw its capacity for exerting control immediately, whereas the priest only saw it belatedly. The priest had not viewed it this way at first, or at times denied he had, and claimed he had no greater designs or intentions for the device he created. It was natural that the lord should see the automaton differently, or it was at least predictable, the priest told us. Given how he judged me in terms of my usefulness, it was unsurprising he would come to see my machine in a similar manner, as an extension of his rule. The lord had always considered his priest to be another lever which he might, from his seat of power, and by small efforts of his own, exert tremendous pressure with over others. As such the lord would remain the operator and the origin of his power, and the priest would be his mechanism, an extension of the arm. But the lord had never entirely trusted his priest, the priest told us, and his mistrust originated from his dim perception of the priest's uncanny power. The lord reckoned that with his priest duly employed he might exact leverage on the public consciousness and augment his other systems of control by way of it. The lord only reckoned this because the lord did not understand the extent to which that leverage, as he saw it, was the foundation of his own power too, that it was the condition of his rule. He thought of the priest as a tool he might pick up and deploy, not realising, so the priest told us, that the priest, or what the priest stood for, was not so much a tool as the idea of having one, and that this was merely one idea alongside many others for which the priest, or the priesthood, had original responsibility. Theirs was a feast of ideas within which the notion of having a tool or not having a tool was a very minor thing indeed. The lord did not know and could never know that the priest, or what the priest stood for, had provided the basic frameworks, the algorithms, the fancies, and the fears, which were the lord's outlook and understanding. His subjects were only biddable to the extent their interiors were enslaved to the conditioning precepts of their religion. The lord could have no knowledge of all this in its extent and purchases. It was beyond his reckoning because it was his conditioning too. And so the lord only suspected some trickery was at work when he felt troubled by his priest. And like his informer, the lord could only conceptualise that trickery as betrayals and counterplots. Yet I suspect even he glimpsed within me the workings of my various soul-making, soul-crushing, civilisational artifices, the priest said. I am convinced when the lord looked at me, he dimly perceived it, although the lord could only consciously express that perception as common suspicion and common dislike and could only attach words to his feeling such as treachery, disloyalty, and breach of trust. This was the basis on which the lord received news of the priest machine. Hearing of it, the lord perceived that it had all the advantages of the priest without the feared betrayals. The priest machine could operate to his advantage without the betraying cunning that the lord so convinced himself of, and which he considered to be the priest's elementary nature. He saw the priest machine as a more predictable agent and a potential improvement on the priest for this reason alone. He thought the priest machine was less likely to double-cross him, and that a machine might even be incapable of deception. This the priest laughed at, given how deception was one of the basic ideas behind the making of the machine. The machine only functioned as it did within the peasant hovel because of its deception, as the informer had reported. That the lord should think the machine incapable of deceiving him only testified to the lord's arrogance, he thought, and his limited imagination. The lord was incapable of placing himself within the world his informer described and for this reason held the machine in higher regard than the priest. But the priest, for his part, also wondered if the priest machine might be an improvement on himself, though for different reasons.

The priest told us it was his sickness at work in the making of the machine. It was, as he put it, the sickness of his divinely instructed consciousness which made him do what he did. It was his ministry employed as it was expressed in his gut. It was the pain of monastic servitude transmitted to his office—a kind of pain accumulated, dripped into all places that will pool it together, turned sour in confinement, rendered in vapours which further befoul the mind—these vapours, he added, can only be produced as a concentrated fog in monasteries. They infect their teachings with every minor privation, curdled, misperceived as virtue, and thrown out for the priesthood to enact. It was the scabbed over denials of the church fathers, he went on, their flesh mortified as their hypocrisies grew, finally venting themselves in the making of something fittingly grotesque. It was the New Testament soaked over the Old, corrupting its fire with its own, greater lie. It was all of that, he suspected, or was it merely fatigue, a kind of mechanical exhaustion, if not a little priestly boredom too, he was always bored, he said. Have I mentioned the fact of my boredom, he asked us.

Boredom suggests the emptiness of existence, the priest explained. No, there is something more, he added. Boredom proves human beings cannot face up to their own emptiness. —It became apparent we were in for another of the priest's digressions. Human beings approach that realisation of their basic emptiness, he went on, and then become bored in the face of it. They very nearly perceive their emptiness and then retreat to a declaration of boredom. Or, at least, they can only experience the emptiness of their lives as such. This declaration of boredom seems to be, on the whole, the very best and most reliable response they can muster before the most abysmal realisation, before the worst thought possible, that nothing, not even this sense of dread, gives human life any kind of value. We must picture these generations of bored spectators, the priest said to us, as they repeatedly confront that abyss, and upon the very precipice declare, *I'm bored.* Those words, he said, are among the most symptomatic utterances of the human animal.

We shuffled a bit and the priest looked at us slyly, asking us which part of his analysis was allowing us to fidget.

Surely you find it extraordinary, he said, that human beings are free of want at last, and then face that state of calm by complaining it bores them to exist that way. The sated condition is one in which the universe has nothing else to offer after the satisfaction of their wants, and they cannot bear it. Here, surely, is no better proof that human life must be some kind of mistake. To suffer with such certainty, and to have been given this respite, only to discover there is nothing but emptiness beyond it, and then, and here is the worst bit, he said, and then to find that emptiness dimly repellent, this is the crowning moment of human absurdity. To yearn for a moment of relief, and then to find that moment faintly unendurable, this really is the consummate glory of an absurd being. It seems the human organism cannot exist at all without suffering for something—and that, he said, precisely that, is its weakness and the origin of its wickedness. It would be better to live for suffering, to strive only for more suffering, he said making these words heavy in his mouth. Or at least to live in suffering and never wish for existence without it. Only that would be less absurd. I am speaking here, he said, of the lowest form of boredom, of course. Only the lowest form of boredom abuts the emptiness of existence. This is the boredom of those who are warm enough but not too warm, sheltered but not imprisoned, and well fed but not overstuffed. For we can become bored in other ways too, he told us. We may be bored with our anger, bored in our pain, but this is only because our anger or our pain has become too familiar, or too predictable, or too often returning, and each has ceased to surprise us. This is not true boredom and only tedium at work. The proper lesson of existence—of the stupidity of human existence—arrives with the boredom of a temporarily sated self. Here listen to me, he said, because I can see you are not yet horrified as you should be. Listen closely now and reckon again with what I am telling you. We suffer for want of food, or water, or security, and find ourselves finally satisfied. We attain, at last, some moments without need or want, and we find that our sated selves are suddenly tired with their lives. We strive for satisfaction and yet when we finally arrive there, we discover there is nothing left to do. We cannot endure this condition where there is nothing immediate making demands upon us, and find that the only way to escape boredom, the priest said, is to begin yearning again, to return from this unendurable pause to the condition of common suffering and ordinary want which propels and distracts us. Can we bring ourselves to any other conclusion regarding the great stupidity of the human animal, he told us. Is there any other reading of the strange pain we feel when we are bored, that yearning after yearning stops. I surely cannot see one.

One of us shifted again, perhaps the taxidermist, and the priest said, but I am not finished yet, rest yourself back on your skins.

Once our ancestors scratched the earth for each bit of food it might give them, he went on. Now we pile the stuff up in granaries. As we are better provided for, we must find new ways to suffer. I foresee a day, he said, when harvests are so regular, and houses so well built, that specialists in human suffering will flog their wares and find willing customers. Meanwhile, the church must take on this growing burden. Why else do we enforce church attendance and inflict its sermons on congregations. And on each Sunday in particular. This so-called day of rest would be the most dangerous day of the week, he added, if we permitted it to remain unfilled by expectation and moral duty, if we allowed it to become a day of true rest, which nobody could endure because it would be a day of true boredom. Without the suffering inflicted by our pews and our sermons and our singing, our people would find other ways to suffer, he said. They would do anything to avoid confronting their own boredom as a weekly event. This boredom would be an argument against existence no philosopher could deliver with equal force. They would rather tear into themselves, or one another, than sit squarely in that day with nothing to distract them from themselves. Rebounding from their boredom, crimes of self-distraction would amass and overflow. Prisons would be filled and break apart as all the horrors of Sunday gone were reckoned. If brought at last to the judge for sentencing, none would manage to reason their violence. That is the potential danger of a Sunday. Its threat of mutinous, anarchic, and dysfunctional revolt against boredom is what necessitates all of the artificial, ordered, and assured suffering of the church. There can be no day of rest otherwise. The church must vitiate the boredom of the day by enforcing suffering of its own. It is a curious fact, he said, that our religion, our religious ancestors, invented the day of rest to justify itself in this way.

The priest spoke, nonetheless, of a higher state of boredom. He said that he suffered from the regularity of his duties, from the repetition at work within scripture—can you imagine how painful it is, he said, to study a book which contains the same story told multiple times. He suffered too from its endless retelling to others, the annual cycle of staid and regulated festivities—no other religion had lacked imagination in this respect so much as his—the yearly re-enactments of the birth and the death of its god all bored him, and the effort he had to make each year to deliver the story of his birth, and the story of his death, with due emetic force, often felt more than he could give. All of which he could not recount without thinking the message of the church, the message he would again discharge, must be intentionally defunct, that it must always at some level fail to heal the existential rift it identified, the suffering it pinpointed, and fail deliberately and by design. The church would fail by worsening the plight of those who listened, for if it did not worsen, if it actually delivered more than minor consolations and moments of respite, it would do itself out of business. This was a crude analysis, he admitted, but too often a crude analysis is rejected for being crude rather than for being false. It was probably idleness too, he said. And his curiosity with it. He found it hard to deny that a large amount of what made him do what he did was idle curiosity. Perhaps it was just his idle curiosity wishing to find out what would happen if he did in fact do what he had recently thought of doing. It was the work of his sick, sick-making curiosity, he suspected, of just wanting to know what would be brought into the world of consequences if he did reproduce himself as a machine—and would anyone notice, indeed. Perhaps this was an experiment of sorts, he went on, and not mere idleness in pursuit of distraction. It was an experiment to discover just what it was they needed of him. He wished to find out what from a peasant perspective goes into the making of a priest. What is a priest at the level of peasant perception, he wondered to himself, so he said to us. I know what I am to myself, but I do not really know what I am to them. It was possible, I thought, that what I am to them is at odds to what I am to myself, and that I might adjust what I am to myself in order to better fit with what I am to them. No, that is not right, he said, correcting himself. I thought that I might adjust what the machine is to itself, so that it matches what I am to them. He looked at us, sitting there in the workshop, and posed the question again, his question which was merely a statement. ——*What is a priest at the level of peasant perception*, he said to us as we listened. What is a priest, and what can be dispensed with because it carries no effects—he said this too. Yes indeed it could be considered an experiment. That thing down there in the corner might be thought of as an instrument of discovery, as a discovering machine, as a voyager in peasant perception. The first priest machine, your prototype, is the conclusion of my enquiry. Can you smell it, he asked us and we nodded, well that smell is the summary of my findings. I wished to find out how much of myself was superfluous and this is what I arrived at. That rotting object in its cowl was the end result of that process, he said, and as he said it I thought he smiled, or wondered if there was an element of mirth in the tone of his voice but could not be sure, my assistant said, falling silent for a while and appearing to wonder as he did if the priest was capable of mirth or not, and if he was capable whether he found some comedy in his discovery, and if he was a laughing anatomist or straight-faced in all of his dissections. Or perhaps this was me wondering that, filling the silence with my own thoughts. Once I had finished stripping myself of anything needless, he continued, this is what I was left with, the priest said. I made the machine to learn if I could do away with large parts of myself, if I could jettison chunks of my priestly nature and still do the work of my visits. I sought to find out if the greater part of my achievements—what others might consider my virtues—were actually defunct or at least needless. If the priest they saw bore little relation to the priest I cultivated, should peasants still be visited by the priest in this fuller sense, he asked, or should peasants be given the priest they saw. He wondered how that priest took shape when he entered their small houses and responded, as he did, to the demand he must visit them. Did the priest they saw have anything to do with the priest he thought himself to be. Did they reckon with his accomplishments, or understand the extent of his training, he continued, and was this why they called him, or was it baser than that. Was it merely an acquired impulse to call the priest and see a priest. And how much of what happened when he visited did he have command of. Or did he do what he did largely in response to what he found there. Could his ministrations in each peasant hovel be as much a creation of the hovel environment as they were a creation of those graceful motions he had been taught to enact. Were his priestly mannerisms and priestly refinements largely generated there with them, and not in his prior, priestly education. Was he, the priest, a product of peasant poverty, peasant idiocy, and peasant bad air, or, at least, was there an element of his priestly nature that was built there, in those places, and so came from the earth and the muck of their living. All of which amounted to an argument against the idea of his intervention, the very notion of intercession. He came to suspect that it was not his intervention which did the work of religion, or not only. It was the work of the priest they saw and not the priest he thought himself to be. The priest they saw was not intervening or interceding but vibrated with the fibres of their perception. His will was not the only will at work he admitted to himself. For indeed, in his perception of himself the magnitude of his will was diminishing. With peasants it was more complicated than a question of his will dominating theirs, bringing light to their pitiful gloam. Their peasant perception was so at odds with his higher priestly perception that it complicated his priestly intervention and perhaps finally annulled it. They did not even establish a mutual pact, a religious compact between his gestures and theirs. His gestures were no longer his from their perception. He came to believe the work of his religion may as much be the work of its benighted converts as it is the work of the priesthood. He suspected the weight of creation probably lay more on their side, so that the religion he thought himself to represent was generated elsewhere and lower down. These peasants in their hovels did not only have an active role in giving body to his religion, filling out its details, furnishing its more feculent parts. Much as he was encouraged by his training to believe religion comes from scripture and higher tradition, if the automaton could be made to work, and if it worked by the power of their outlooks and their projections, the true engine of his religion must be found within the peasant experience itself. He came to think that when you saw a peasant engaged in the basest activities, you were actually watching a religion at work. A peasant emptying a stie, a peasant feeding a chicken or a child, a peasant holding a chamber pot, or a peasant pissing in a ditch has the basic elements of religion in hand. When the local lord strikes a peasant down with his cudgel—as he has been known to do—that peasant raises his hands and holds his head and carries there, in those blooded fingers, the basis of religious feeling. All I present them with is a malleable icon in the form of a man, a set of materials, my robes, my book, to which they can attach themselves and their religious intuition. So yes. It was an experiment, then, he said, or it became an experiment in which he wished to find out if what they needed of him could be simulated, and if a selective repetition of particular, identified features and gestures could still deliver them of their lives to the gentle panic of religious feeling. He sought to design his machine so it might carry them from the occasional upsurges of pain and suffering which beset them, to an extended, constantly present, and more carefully managed state of existential angst. Some of this thinking informed the initial conception, he thought, although he still could not quite recall how, precisely, he went about constructing the first figure, the prototype, which he dressed as he would dress, disguising it with his familiar habit and cowl. This priest had always dressed the part of the monk. His was the drama of the monk who has wandered too far from the monastery and become lost in the world. Or, if not lost, so burdened with life beyond the monastery he was unable to drag himself back inside. This wandering monk has at last made do with things—I will make do with all this, he says of the world around him, and adopt the life and labour of the priest. It was obvious to us that he had no interest at all in the making of the second priest machine, and that he produced the second automaton purely on the lord's orders. The priest said he considered his experiment finished, and that he had found out what he expected to find. For the second priest machine he was given all available resources. These included access to the lord's abattoir and the first inspection of all offcuts and skins, as well as the services of the lord's personal taxidermist. This cutter, stitcher, and stuffer was temporarily released from filling the lord's mansion—a minor castle—with the heads of beasts projected from its inner walls, lining its halls and corridors and landings and stairways. To any other creature it was a mausoleum. There were other recruits too. The land surveyor's assistant was engaged as the second apprentice, together with a trainee horologist—the clockmaker—who would see to the smaller devices involving cogs and springs and suchlike things. Evidently the second automaton was to be far more sophisticated. Although the priest could not precisely recall his motivations in regard of the first automaton—and filled our ears instead with speculations— in relation to the second he was more certain. By the time of the second figure, he was glad to be shot of his priestly duties. His duties largely involved giving consolation, he said. Basically, a priest is a consoling machine, he told us. Or a machine for giving the appearance of consolation. Priestly training is largely oriented towards this effect, he said. Priests learn consoling gestures, consoling looks, and the different tones of a consoling voice. When priests give consolation, what they deliver is merely the appearance of giving consolation. That is what consolation amounts to when you receive a priest into your household and have him say something to put your mind at rest. And behind the appearance of giving consolation is a lesson, he went on. All so-called priestly consolations are lessons, and the lesson is always the same. The priest gives only one lesson, he told us, the lesson of human suffering, and so it is that these are not consolations at all. Viewed properly they are not even failed consolations, he said. These are not attempted consolations that fail in their effort. So-called priestly consolations but serve only as vehicles for the priestly lesson. A priest is called upon to console, and each consolation is but another lesson in suffering. This, in the fuller sense, is what the priest meant by calling his consolations mere appearances of consolation, although he wondered what true, non-priestly consolation looked like and if true consolation had ever existed on earth. You might judge my consolations badly, the priest said to us as we sat in the workshop and listened, but does true consolation exist. Ask yourselves that. Has anyone ever truly consoled anyone else, he said to us, leaning in towards us as he did so and looking at us very closely as he said it. Can consolation exist, he declared. On this earth, he added. The priest told us this, my assistant told me, and the priest told us much else as he sat before us as our model and our muse. He had spent already too much of his life giving cause and purpose to what he described as the unceasing reign of pain and diminishment. He was tired of teaching its necessity to others, and by teaching it, suffering it himself in the form of heightened perception. He said when he taught the needfulness of pain, and when he taught that pain was just as much the work of divine intent as was pleasure, he raised that lesson within his own perception of the world. He said that he took his lesson and turned it inward. He said this lesson regarding the necessity of suffering influenced how he experienced his own discomforts, and that this influence was unavoidable. He said he had lost the ability to experience his own suffering without that lesson, and he did not have unfiltered access to his own pain. He said he was molested by his words as much as he molested others with them. The priest said it only caused him further suffering to explain their suffering—and that he took no pleasure in it—even though his suffering was of a higher sort, arranged on a higher plane, a level to which he hauled them, and to which they rose by small increments. They approached the heights of his perception, he said, to the extent they heard what he had to say. And they understood his lesson by degrees. Still, the priest said, they only approached the lower heights, the foothills if you like, and rarely made it up beyond the treeline into the zone of clearer air, purer perception, and more evident desolation. Peasants cannot see the point of mountaineering, he said. They stay below with their bad air. Their peasant perception might be likened to a fog which creeps into the lower valleys and overcomes the lower hills, leaving those few who have climbed higher entirely cut off from one another on their island peaks. Or so my assistant recounted as we walked. He claimed that this was all what the priest had told him, perhaps not word for word, but along those lines.

The priest came down to the workshop, he said, and spoke to us about his former motivations and about the building of his first automaton. He came down to us from his chambers only when small adjustments to the second automaton—always deteriorating—were again required. Otherwise the priest was free of its maintenance. The priest sat in his chambers above us, or on the westward balcony. He wrote and spoke and complained at the horizon, telling the sun to set and not return until the earth was done of its people. The priest had lent his greater insight and indeed his own composition—this is to say, the structure of his bearing—to the initial design of the second automaton, giving himself to its basic conception and spiritual effects. He delegated the rest of the work to his first apprentice, and via that first delegate to my own self, the second apprentice, and then to the real innovators, the taxidermist, and the horologist, who for their part were content to be commanded—they had enough to deal with in the making of their devices. We did not know where the priest found his first apprentice—the first apprentice never said anything about himself as if he were born the very moment the priest recruited him—but we suspected the first apprentice had previously worked for the lord, that he performed some low duties in his household, and was entirely unregarded in his former life. In his new position, appointed as he was as the priest's chief delegate and as the chief supervisor of his workshop, the first apprentice oversaw his dominion with the narrow determination of an overlooked man who has at last been given some measure of command over his fellow beings. These were not the precise words used to describe him. My assistant, the land surveyor wrote, did not describe the first apprentice in this way, but set out the basic features of the man with sufficient detail for me to see what he was.

My assistant used different words, and with them constructed a less perceptive, less penetrating version of the first apprentice he had known and worked under. But as he did so I could see in my own recollection similar men, and occasionally women, whom I have also known and have sometimes suffered myself in all their great, stupefying small-mindedness. Overlooked creatures are the pettiest enactors of rules when finally given some command over them. They punish minor infractions with the kind of diligence years of living at the receiving end will afford. And if most people, in most times and places, have considered themselves overlooked in small or large part, most of them, when given some position of authority, will observe the command to organise others as if it were their originary calling. They will see their new position of influence as evidence of their empowerment, as a place from which to exert control over others—with malice, or malice disguised as tenderness—as if they could at last invest the world with their own hitherto thwarted will and reasonableness. These overlooked creatures, seemingly trusted, seemingly able to wield power, take up their position with satisfaction and a sense of entitlement. They cannot see that their outlook is in actual fact an acquired outlook, and that their independence of decision is a fabricated independence, and that their position of command is a fabricated command. They will not see that their outlook, that the outlook of the petty ruler, was manufactured for them by other petty rulers who suffered that outlook before them, and that this is how one petty ruler establishes the conditions for the next and so passes on their enslavement. My assistant is fortunate I am not one of them, I thought, as we waited at the edge of the clearing to see if they would emerge from their huts. My assistant is extremely lucky, I thought to myself as we loitered there, very lucky indeed I am not one of these petty-minded fools. As we stood and as he gently dropped the rods I had placed in his arms, I told myself how blessed I was with self-control, with not needing to exert power over others. I have always paused before exerting my will and held back before having something to say. I have always felt it necessary to let others have their mistakes for themselves, I thought, as I heard the rods clatter to the ground at his feet. I have always looked at those around me and remained silent so long as I could to see them suffer from themselves without my intervention. My patience is celestial. I see the contours of their mistakes before they make them, this in truth is my land surveyor's gaze, and I watch those mistakes materialise with the satisfaction of being right in my predictions. Soon enough I would see his mistake materialise, the mistake of not holding the rods tightly, deliberately, the mistake of his inattention. We had been waiting there from first light and could see as we arrived the glow of their oil lamps that leaked under the door. The trees around us creaked and moaned—no wood is ever still or silent but this one had denied us sleep. And yet, above its lumbered agonies we could discern the faint sound of the ropes as they were still wound and tightened. It seemed they had been working all night, treading the rope walks, weaving their yarns and strands and first narrow cords into a cable of necessary girth. Perhaps they worked as the two men we had seen, and used similar techniques, and yet they were better equipped, longer trained, and more accomplished. The benefits of a larger workforce, improved tools, longer rope walks, and better functioning spinning wheels. More tension, greater torque. At some point the two men we had seen before out in the open, in the valley above, did indeed arrive with the narrow cord they had made. It surprised me, perhaps it did, to see them. They entered the clearing before the huts, hauling a small rock by that fresh line of rope as if to indicate its strength. On their backs they carried bundles of raw, unbludgeoned hemp. The first man reached the door of the furthest hut and called out—we could not decipher it—and the door was opened. The two arrivals stood for some moments, strip lit by the oil lamps, heads upright to their audience within the hut, and then each man outside turned to the rock they had brought, gesturing at it, gesturing at the cord, holding the cord up for inspection, holding it slack and then taut between their hands, and seeking admission by way of it, or so it seemed to me. But admission was not granted. They were asked to hand their raw hemp in at the doorway, we could not see the hands which received it. For their part the two men received nothing in return. The door was drawn back into its casement, and they were left standing alone with their freshly woven but narrow cord and the small rock they had brought there by way of it. Dropping the rope, they left soon after in the direction of the higher valley. Finally, the door of another hut several buildings in was opened, and a line of rift valley dwellers emerged, hoisting their own greater rope from one shoulder to the next. It was a cable of sufficient girth to dredge an ocean trench. A hawser thick enough to haul a ship from its surface. But much shorter, and so oddly stout in its dimensions. I came to think it more resembled a reticulated python than a rope. A python fatted on its own kind. A hawser glutted with python children, python rivals, and python neighbours, lined parallel and eaten whole. There in the yard before the doors they paused with the cable hung between them, as several others emerged behind carrying sacks—hemp sackcloth sacks—hanging these sacks on their own shoulders, less heavily but not without effort. These were filled with supplies, we discovered, and those supplies were mainly the tubers they ate, their main diet—it would soon be ours. I walked into the clearing before the huts and announced myself. The hauling of the rope stopped, and they regarded me for some moments after which I announced myself again, indicating my assistant now too, and told them we were come in search of a boulder, rumoured to be somewhere further down the valley, and that we understood it had some significance to them, and could we see it. We had been given to believe the boulder was of considerable size, and yet they were able to drag the thing, so it was said, and had been dragging at it for an extended period, for years perhaps, and could we ask why, and would they be able to tell us more about it.

The rift valley dwellers have given nothing away. They haul the rope by day and coil it around their encampment, end-to-end, when the valley falls dark. We have remained with them despite their slow pace to be sure of our route into the cut. My assistant has been quiet for three days now. He seems entranced by the rope. We sleep with them at night within the rope circle. He rests his ear against the ouroboros and listens.

They have given up holding the rope at the shoulder and drag it along the ground. Their shoulders are raw from the carrying and glisten each evening in the firelight. When my assistant rests his ear, he listens to the muck.

Last night a group of rift valley dwellers arrived from further down the canyon and joined our encampment.

Today they helped haul the rope with the rest of the group. It is returned to shoulder height. I suspect we are now nearing the boulder.

No trees grow in the vicinity of the boulder which is well below sea level. It is likely the sun only casts directly into the valley here a few times each year, if that, and certainly never from overhead, even at this latitude. The sides are almost sheer. The upper valley—gentle at first— had narrowed and deepened, as we had seen, and from there at last fallen into its fissure as water draining from a crack. It is no exaggeration, I think, to state that the rift thereafter abandoned the recognisable contours of known topography. None of the books I have studied, nor charts or illustrations I have seen, nor traveller's accounts I have read, have described anything remotely close to the nature of this rift. I fear my own description must fail to render it. My records of the elevations descended—elevations which have become depths—my sketches, such as they are, do not add to the compendium of known earthly formations. They would seem to refute them. I am reduced to very basic observations which do not at all touch the peculiarity of my experience. Such as the disappearance of the river. It is possible to note that absence and be understood in regard of it, to be heard declaring the merest fact of its absence. But about the nature of it not being there, I can say nothing cogent. It seems to me the departed river has left a path it might otherwise have taken, the long black slick of a void that carries not water but the lack of water deeper into the earth. It is, as I say, inexpressible. And so, I record that the river water itself—never deep or broad—had disappeared entirely, probably run off into a side-chamber further up. From there on in, its travel must remain unknown. Onward to a subterranean sea, perhaps. Or to pressure domes where at intervals the water is forced up to the surface in gushing ventricles. Or to some terminus underground where the waters of the river are simply left to diffuse and permeate those rocks which exist in that frigid, intermediate zone between the heat of the core and the heat of the sun. Why the river should not run on in the cut perplexed me, since it was still wet underfoot, and water was able to pool and trickle and yet it would not accumulate and flow. As we arrived, I directed my questions to the creature who was, at that point, and would remain, crouched on its leading edge—for the boulder had its very own stylite. She was sat on her haunches above us, palms laid flat against the stone, impassive before the spectacle of our arrival, intent in her focus. We moved and motioned. I walked backwards to what must have been the centre of her gaze and addressed her once more with questions concerning the boulder, about why she sat there, and where had the boulder come from, and what was its significance, and where were they hauling it to. She closed one eye, and then the other, shifting me against her horizon, or so I thought, by a minor parallactic degree. At last, after having me shudder for some moments in her vision, and seeing that I would not be shifted, she stared intently at me with both eyes, and did so without blinking any further. Finally, I abandoned this attempt to raise her attention and turned my own to the boulder beneath her. My profession is, after all, a watchful one. It translates distances and heights and angles into sleepless figures and tells the earth as it cannot otherwise be seen. If the dimensions of the rift had caused me to doubt my instruments, the boulder reassured them. Leaving my assistant with the ranging rods, the staff, the tripod, and even the theodolite—I was quite relaxed on

that front, long assured he would never meddle with it—I
walked the edges of the boulder to estimate its length, and
then its circumference. I would measure it properly later,
but for the moment my land surveyor's stride, developed
over the years to a near-perfect three feet, would gather
its basic particulars. My best comparison of its size and
dimension would be the proportions of a whale, the kind
I have seen beached submitting breathlessly to its weight,
and yet, unlike the whale this boulder tapered early to the
blunt point of its rear, that node raised in mid-air as if the
beast were stranded in its last attempt at return, the tail
fins already lost. The boulder broadened fairly uniformly
from there, this nib, to its highest moment and its greatest
girth. The lower edges of the rock were carved—these
indentations may have been representational, hieroglyphs
of a sort—with the lines and curves gathering together to
produce the chaos of inscription—or so it struck me—
which was its front. The carvings were not fresh but run
over at their edges as if successive fingers over many years
had wandered along their lines, fingers following each
inflection and every downward turn. Beyond my reach,
which must itself be over the reach of most, the boulder
was not at all marked and the stylite had the surface as
it was above in its natural rough condition. Hers was the
geological surface, theirs was the representational one. The
ropes extended across the full circumference, some around
the base, others tethered from the nib forwards, generating
a stretched web of interlocking lines around its equator with
multiple mooring points from which the hauling ropes fell
slack. The rift valley dwellers were arranged around a fire
nearby on which they roasted the tuber of that plant, better
harvested higher up the valley, each uniquely shaped nodule
impaled on its own long stick and held out to steam and

crust over, which was how they cooked. We joined them with sticks and tubers of our own, using the point like an auger as we had seen them do, gouging out the inner flesh of the nodule, hard and unyielding in its uncooked state. I saw them dig this harvest some strides from the boulder and when they left took one of the rods and levered out my own small harvest from the earth which had given so little of itself to the crop. There was scant light to grow with. It was a pitiful return, or so I thought, but it sustained them, and would have to sustain us too, for I had seen them eat nothing else.

The priest said that before his work on the first automaton, or perhaps because of it, he had come to doubt the basic idea said to underpin the workings of his religion and its pagan antecedents, namely, the notion humans must be presented with a framework which gives cause and meaning to their pain. Worse still, the priest felt, was the accompanying argument which claims humanity has grown to such a weak condition that without such a framework these same individuals would decide they were done with living and rather would do away with each other and themselves, or at least wish it that way, as if they were not already doing that, doing one another in and doing themselves over with the frameworks they still possessed. It did not matter what the framework of understanding was, or how the activity of sense-giving worked. It mattered far more that it existed, he said, now repeating the argument he had grown to doubt. These latter-day humans needed to see there was some kind of organising intention behind the violences they suffered and submitted themselves to. There had to be some kind of systemic or repetitive arrangement of forces and externally appointed stimuli which served, even in their great injustices, to reassure individual beings their pain was at least predictable and had some observable cause. What else, so the argument went, are pleas for justice and reparation but systems for categorizing evil. What else is each demand that the world be rectified but the continued assertion that violences can be read, that they are legible, amid their chaos. The desire for justice is merely a demand for legible pain, he said. They would be done with the world, so the argument went, he said, and so I once believed, if they discovered the vast bulk of pain is accidental and without meaning. They would be done with the entire system, their entire outlook, and so too they would be done with themselves, because they could no longer reckon in their pain, and would as a result seek to end it, at last having arrived at the final dramatic proclamation of an indignant consciousness—a suicidal nihilism, a terminal pessimism— where apparently nothing is more unbearable to the human outlook than the spectacle of one's own suffering shorn of any kind of signification. The priest laughed at this now as he said it, and the workshop resounded with the noise of him laughing. This noise he made then ceased abruptly as if he had just noticed the sound he created. He had come to find all of it, he said, this entire sequence of argument, to be profoundly unconvincing if not also a joke of its convictions. The final solution to human suffering it proclaimed—this wilful self-annihilation—was doubtful to the extent that suicide is rarely enacted as a decision but proceeds more often from a kind of exhaustion with living. Suicide is not the triumph of will but its collapse, he said. This exhaustion drains the brain of its energies and reduces volition to a shade of its earlier flame. The suicidal outlook is, more often than not, the outlook and the demeanour of a creature which has become slumped. It is not the outlook of an organism that raises itself to the full force of some inbuilt, self-destructive power, realising at last that nothing can justify its pain, as if it can then declare—well then let's end it all. He laughed again at this, and it seemed as though his first automaton, hooded and bent over in the corner, shifted a little to the sound of it. Again, the priest snapped his mouth shut to the noise of his laughter, and continued, but over and above these reflections on the matter of suicide—a business in which he had dealt with tiresome regularity during his ministries—the priest simply could not fathom the conceit which held that humans are, or at least have become in their fundamentals, sense-making creatures, and that they bow before their reverence for truth to such an extent, indeed, that when sense and signification are stripped out, the lack of sense itself is felt to be a crime on the level of, or even worse than, the unbearable persistence of their pain. These humans, these so-called meaning-makers, would rather hurl themselves into space than live in a world they could only experience as a void. Or, more probably, so the argument goes, they would continue to look for meaning anywhere, at any price, rather than confront its absence. The priest said he had of course often wondered himself why he went on living. It was clear to him that his religion did once play a role at a higher level, soothing him with its proclaimed transcendence, as did the mechanics of observance furnish him at a lower, more quotidian plane of his existence with the impetus to keep going, helping him, or at least distracting him from the question of why he must continue to live. He was sure nonetheless that he had never asked the question with the kind of painful seriousness it perhaps warranted, where the wrong answer, or perhaps the correct but unwished-for answer, would have some kind of lasting effect, and would not merely feed his curiosity as all answers had hitherto done. The priest told us that in the end it was the wound itself which compelled him to live. By which he meant that he would repeatedly wound himself, mainly by thinking things about himself which hurt him acutely—although in principle a persistent flesh wound would work just as well—because as he attended to his wounds and inspected the hurt he caused, as he marvelled at the pain and sought to close each rupture, indeed, as he simply felt his lacerated flesh and his lacerated mind, he found himself compelled to exist as such. He experienced his pain as a compulsive force which drew him onward from one day to the next. It was his vital drive, his propulsion mechanism. Pain was his engine, the priest told us. He knew that, and so he cultivated it, but anyone who lives must be propelled in just the same way, he thought. This caused him to wonder again at the needlessness, the baroque architecture of the consolations he had learnt as a priest to offer others, the lessons in suffering he had been taught to give, when merely attending to the situation of a wound could give meaning or at least propulsion to existence, could produce acute sensations which focused the mind on its own urgent presence within the world. This all amounted to saying that it seemed to him entirely futile, and certainly an indulgence, to wonder what he was doing in life, why he had come to exist as he did, and how, perhaps, he might live differently, when all he needed in order to proceed was to attend to the immediate experiences of living in a lacerating world, a universe which had no regard of his existence within it. And so it was that ever since the automaton, or around the time of its conception, he had simply stopped wondering about the needfulness of a meaningful world, had lived on without thinking any more about it, and could report it was quite possible to live like that, and there was nothing extraordinary about it. He said this to us all, but directed his comments mostly at the horologist, perhaps because the horologist was most likely to understand, or perhaps because he most needed to hear it, spending his own life, as he did, attending to mechanisms—their wheels, pallets, ratchets, and pinions—whose continued motion he was responsible for assuring. Many years had passed, the priest said, since his religion had nourished him, if it ever had, and thereby propelled him further onward and inward. But the idea that life must be given meaning, if only at a very basic level, remained parasitic within him and seemed as though it could not be driven out. His faith retired but this residuum stayed. He said that he flayed himself with it and thereby flayed the residuum that remained within him. He told us that the best way of dealing with this residuum was to turn it into a weapon and then turn that weapon against itself. Enduring regard of the activity of sense-making far outlived his faith, he said, and remained its most assured legacy, its still-originating engine for all his higher discomforts—the location of the refined and exalted wound. He sat there, saying this under our inspections as we remodelled the decayed temples of the second automaton, which, as we observed, pulsated with a faint tremor. Boethius was executed by way of the temples, he told us with a wink. The temples crush inward more easily than the rest of the skull. We came very close so as to inspect his own temples, we lent in so we could fully appreciate their faint movements, and the horologist and taxidermist then wondered aloud about their reproduction, about which mechanisms and skins would best repeat the effect. Then they fell silent again, as the priest spoke to us a little more of these things, and other matters concerning the pursuit of suffering and signification. The priest said he did of course recognise the irony of his position in explaining this to us, as we lent in more closely still to further observe the palpitations at the side of his skull. But the priest assured us that he pursued it nonetheless, and that he had also lived it to some extent. Yes indeed, he was willing to admit, perhaps all that time spent above in his chamber these days, writing about the full extent of human suffering and pain, was time spent in ironic production. All that time he had used up—time he would never get back—writing about the fact that we must surely manage to exist, as surely we do, without any ultimate sanction, whereupon pain must remain always to an extent inexplicable, and that we can and do easily live with this fact of it being impossible to reason out, and so on and so forth, was time spent in a kind of futile labour. He admitted that all those descriptions in his notepads in the chambers above our workshop, all of this writing and thinking of his, was a further enactment of the sense-making apparatus the full force of which he was attempting to deny, or at least strip of its promises. All his scribbling about suffering is another form of exploitation, he said, where pain is again co-opted to the activity of the so-called intellect. All he thought, all his thinking, could never release itself entirely from the acquired habit to justify existence, or at least set it out in its basic contours, or make it bearable by reducing it to an aspect of cognition. A lapsed priest such as himself still could not pass up any opportunity to make an interesting spectacle of pain. Even raising the spectre of human pain as a basic enigma, as a fundamentally inexplicable phenomenon, still served, he was prepared to admit, to further that preoccupation with explicating or at least fixating on, and recording, its presence. One way or another, suffering was still placed within the order of things, divinely sanctioned at one end—as a means to tutelage—or fundamentally enigmatic at the other, said to be meaningless but still given meaning by that gesture. And as the priest said this, he held one fist in the other and we saw his nails dig in at the back of the hand. Irreligious observers of pain are in some respects its very worst and most beguiling servants, he told us. He had no doubt, then, that in some sense it was right to say our obsession with human misery still rules us, but he still held very closely to the point, which was his basic argument, that this admission is not the same as declaring our preoccupation with thinking about suffering, with producing it and declaring against it, governs us entirely. I refuse to believe, he declared, that humans have indeed reached that high point of abstract intellectualism—because this, surely, is what we are talking about here—whereafter the moment in which that intellectual project fails and ceases to deliver meaning, the entire edifice falls. There is, moreover, he told us, a shadow belief which exists behind the presumption I have just laboured against, namely the idea that if we can only avoid this suicidal nihilism, we can reach beyond it, or perhaps reach backward in time to that age before the contrivances existed which spawned this need of explanation. We would have to extend our grasp back very far, he admitted, much further than these very first attempts to burden the world with meaning. This, he told us, is the dream, unstated, but widely felt, that we could return ourselves to the era of mankind's great cheerfulness. That we could bring about once more the time of free, innocent pleasure, when humanity was first happy, if not a little simple, perceiving the world before it was given weight—which is to say, before it was given depths beyond immediate experience. This was a time before pessimism set down its roots in human consciousness, he said. This pessimism, still yet to appear, would only ever be produced by each betrayal of the promise of meaning. This pessimism only ever existed as the after-effect of the desire for truth. He confessed there was a time of his own, within his own life, when he hoped for something like the unattenuated happiness he imagined, and that he trained for it, denying every reason, every value, every justification that weighed down his perception, but that what he felt, at last, was the evacuation of his spirits. He became unfeeling towards himself, which is not to say he no longer felt. Without that feeling which was ordinarily the grounds of his perception he could not see himself nor judge what he became. Still, he did not discount the possibility that this sensation he arrived at may indeed be what the originary cheerfulness once felt like. If this was originary cheerfulness, he said, it had none of the connotations that have since accumulated around the word. All subsequent notions which have described the cheery outlook, or the cheery disposition, bore little relation to what he felt in this evacuated state. He came to believe that what we now think of as a cheerful experience, what we have since convinced ourselves of as a desirable object, is just another epiphenomenon of human artifice, put to work, like all other artifices, to keep societies in the conditions of their enslavement. Human beings in the form they have now taken, he said to us, actually consent to the imperium of good cheer as another means to manipulate and regulate one another. The cheerful state I experienced—the evacuation I achieved—was nothing to do with how cheerfulness is now somehow presented, he said, that is to say, as a so-called happy condition, a natural state of lightness, into which well-disposed and lucky people will let themselves slip, and within which, for as long as it lasts, they may exist in the pleasurable myopia, the fully uncontrived, carefree abandon of their experience. Good cheer, he told us, actually happens to be one of the most contrived yet successfully self-concealing agents of human coercion he had yet come across. Almost all forms of laughter too he treated with suspicion, so he went on, as more or less proximate imitations of the laughter of very small infants, itself an invention, and not original to birth, because new-borns never laugh and will at best only shriek that inimitable new-born cry. This early laughter, which develops later, and after some weeks or months, seemed to him less consciously manipulative, perhaps entirely selfless at first, and yet would grow alongside the teachings of selfhood to become the acquired laughing-habit of adulthood, and often enough too, a conscious performance, a deliberately enacted (and thereby doubly horrific) mirth. There was a particular laugh he tolerated for many years but eventually came to utterly despise, a form of animal barking, he called it. The head is cast back, the jaw held wide and pulsating with the neck. The bark is thrown out to the air above as if anyone could be mistaken that this laughter was an involuntary outburst, more forceful than most, and so, or so the effect is supposed to be, or so one is supposed to assume, this laughter, this specific outburst, is presumably more genuinely mirthful than ordinary laughter, which is hardly itself wanting for happiness, so it seems. Such laughter—he called it emetic laughter—when practiced in moderation, wishes to signify the fundamental cheerfulness of character, the spiritual health, the elemental levity, which apparently courses through that sound and the person who makes it, where indeed, he said, this very gesture is in actuality, he told us, nothing but, and should be further understood as another symptom of spiritual ill-health, a further inversion of the soul against the organism, the last, most dismal sound of humanity's great, unquenchable pessimism.

At dawn the activity resumes in exactly the same way it did the previous dawn and the dawn before that. The rift valley dwellers make first for the sludge pit that lies some yards away from the hauling point. Here they urinate. The pit has otherwise already filled overnight from a network of narrow drainage channels which draw water from the land about the boulder. Shallow at first in the immediate vicinity of the rock, these long depressions take form as elongated puddles, gathering moisture from the upper layers of the mud. As they depart from the region around the boulder, the channels then draw down into themselves to become narrow cuts nearly a foot in depth and far less than a foot in width, looping from the land they drain, then gathering together as they mass towards the pit. Here the channels shallow out at last, forming a small delta, leaking water over its lower rim. At the other end is the pump. Two Egyptian screws of the sort described by Archimedes extend from the very base of the pit and rise at an angle parallel to one another, reaching far above its upper rim to an arrangement of wooden gutters which take any water wound upwards far away from the region of the boulder. Several among them will slide down into the pit and begin work at the base of each screw. Others leave to maintain the drainage channels. The water which was drawn overnight from the land about the boulder brings with it a heavy silt. This they dig at with wooden spades. Those who stand at the base of the pit, in the silt and water which holds about knee and thigh, work hard to free the lower part of each screw as best they can, flinging spadefuls of the slurry over the rim where it flattens out with its wetness and leaks small rivulets of grey water across the earth. The digging points at the base of each screw are now largely filled with turbid but movable water. Those who dig there further broaden this area of water at the bottom of the pit even as the silt moves to backfill their work. They do this just as others begin to clamber onto each screw and set their feet into the treading points that are cut around the coil. With three to a screw and a further two valley dwellers at the connecting wheel, they pause for a moment and breathe inward, poised for the great force, the considerable effort it will take to commence the turning. Another who stands nearby announces with the blunt noise of their speech, and those at the screw heave it into motion. Over at the boulder the rest will now be inspecting the ropes, still slack, but held above the ground and lifted from the wetness upon short, stout crutches. These were driven into the sodden earth the night before as the ropes were relaxed. The stylite remains in place, having slept in the same position on her haunches. Now awakened, she oversees the activity again— the difference between the waking and the sleeping state is the opening of an eye. Supervised like this, they line each major rope and prepare to lift. As with the screw, they hold themselves poised for some moments, braced for the effort they will give. The stylite raises her gaze from the rock, draws her lips back to the gums, and exhales a short, rasping breath, the announcement to lift the rope, which they do at once. Then she draws her lips back a second time, exhales again, and they begin the pulling. The rope line lengthens as it grows taut and the weave unwinds slightly between their grasping hands, whitened, and stretched where skin and rope meet. The mud is still very wet under their feet, their soles bound in bark and straw taken from the upper reaches of the valley on which the sun still fell. But the mud is not as sodden as it would have been, I assume, without the activity of drainage. On that first day my assistant and I stood and watched, or at least I watched and my assistant talked, expecting as I did some kind of perceptible movement to result from their efforts which were spurred and spurred again as directed by the stylite. At last they laid their ropes on the wooden crutches and unbent their backs to the grey strip above. After a while the stylite exhaled and the pulling resumed. I laid a small stick on the ground a finger width away from the leading edge of the boulder. This I managed during one of their pauses and then retreated as they resumed, returning to look at the stick during the next pause, and returning again within several pauses after that to measure the gap. I could detect no difference. They laid the ropes on crutches and I came back in. Nothing. The stick was still a finger width from the leading edge. This places in context the efforts just expended with all adults engaged in the hauling. I returned to the rear of the boulder, which was slightly better lit than on the evening of our arrival but was still cloaked in the twilight of the rift, and submitted the immediate vicinity to a closer inspection. The vegetation is diminutive this far down the cut—mainly liverworts and ferns and other primitives. Trees no longer grow here having nothing much to stretch for. The wood they burn, the sticks they hold their tubers with, all of this has been brought down from higher up. Given the slow rate of growth due to the poor conditions just noted, I was struck by how close these plants followed the boulder, some of the bryophytes even reaching near enough to almost touch its rear edge. The first ferns, which were themselves not far behind the first bryophytes, were already thick at the base and had clearly been growing there for a number of years. These ferns, I remember thinking, have been growing and dying back upon their delicate stumps for some time. I reached for a ranging rod and gouged the earth. In its consistency and colour this earth behind the boulder is very similar to the muck that is trampled before it and which coats their feet and fills the drainage channels with its silt. The mud is grey and tends to hold its shape even when partly dried through handling. But a mere handspan beyond this a layer of organic matter has accumulated. This composition falls apart in the palm, and a further handspan after that my augur could not reach the base of it. Decayed organic matter lies very thickly here—the remains of past ferns as well as worts and mosses and other non-vasculars. Given the diminishment of decaying leaves and stems to their skeletal outlines and from those outlines to the very smallest traces, a thick accumulation of organic remains or even just a thin coating should be taken as the sign of the passage of years and not months or weeks. All things considered there was little evidence as far as I could see that the boulder had recently moved, not by any substantial margin, and if it had just been drawn a little forward, its advance in that direction had been minor, a hairsbreadth perhaps, and so of no distance which I with my surveying gear was equipped to record. What I could see clear evidence of, nonetheless, was a deep furrow extending back into the thicker vegetation which approximated the width of the boulder at its widest point. We would follow that later, I decided. When we are done here, we will go see where the furrow leads, I thought, as I set about arranging my equipment, assembling the theodolite on its tripod, unpacking the various tape measures I carried, and all the other equipment which are the surveyor's essentials. My assistant still would not yield to my instructions and so I had to use my usual surveyor's ingenuity to find purchase points for the end of my tape in all the various crevices and places I would usually look for to anchor it. My activities around the boulder did seem indeed to impact upon them. I felt certain there was some impact here, and that my impact could be discerned. My presence had some influence on the concentration of those assembled, and, by consequence, on their ability to haul the rope without breaking effort. I could sense they might falter at any point, and that it was because of my being there that they might do this, or perhaps I could sense they wished only to pause to look up and return my stare, although they never did. It was impossible to tell but I was sure their concentration was affected. I had no datum mark, having never seen those before me without them knowing me to be looking. But it was reasonable to assume my presence affected them because of the stylite. I could safely reckon that my being there had some kind of sway upon their work, I thought, and upon their understanding of their work, and upon their understanding of themselves before the work they performed. I knew this because of how she observed me when I walked in the range of her stare. The stylite looked at me with something approaching venom, I thought. When I walked across her gaze, I felt that venom from her unshifting eyes. Her attention was, if anything, strengthened and not diminished by my distractions. Her annoyance could be seen in the determination of her looking. It was unlikely they had suffered visitors much, if at all, and their daily ritual seemed to have nothing to mark or interrupt its progress, only the waxing and waning gloom of the rift valley. This is the extent of its day. There are no seasons or other activities so far as I can see that might bring the rhythms and the accidents of the world to bear upon their lives. There are no intrusions here, unlike above where a flat horizon brings the possibility of approach from every angle. Here it is a question of further up or further down, of turning one way or right round to the other. Their activity is only punctured by the occasional migration for materials and harvests and work in the rope-binding huts where the rift is still wooded. Their children are present each day at the boulder, and sit inactive, watching the rope and the work of their parents and grandparents, learning all they need to know about their lives in the trench as they hunch and look, acquiring their lesson from the spectacle before them. Childhood in the trench is directed just as its linear possibilities are arranged, oriented towards the higher task of haulage, or the alternative path, which was downward further into the rift and involves retreat and diminishment and premature disposal. Where they disposed of their children, I could not tell. Not even the adults whose remains are larger had burial sites so far as I could see. No stones, no mounds. I went to the rock and hammered a horizontal line with an arrow pointing upwards from below. This has served as my datum mark. The children did not respond to the sound of my chiselling or seemed not to hear it. For some time after I attempted to arrange my assistant with the levelling staff and rods so I could begin to triangulate outwards from the boulder and draw my first plans of its near vicinity. He was, unsurprisingly, far worse at holding the staff vertical—and still—than he was at holding the entire bundle of rods and walking with them. Some of it I could manage by myself at those places where I was able to drive a ranging rod into the ground. I would set each rod up and measure its elevation from the vantage of my theodolite. It was laborious, walking backward each time to the rod to reposition it, where a proper assistant might have moved the rod or the staff in response to a simple gesture from myself, or a few commands from where I stood at the tripod, and would have taken the tape with him too. It was worth having an assistant for this, so that I might note down the new distance without walking, rearranging the rod, tracing the line back with the tape, reading the distance, noting the new angle from the scope, and then returning once more to the rod to unhook the tape and move it to its next position. I need a boy, I said, walking towards them. I had exhausted my patience with the rods. A boy, I repeated, pointing to a few likely candidates. I need a boy, I said again, saying this as I did with my assistant standing by my side, his incessant recounting once more resumed. One of you, I went on. I need one of you, I said again slightly raising my voice against the background of his telling. I looked at them with a commanding stare. One of you will come with me, I said at last decisively. The several boys I had in mind, reasonably well proportioned, I thought, steady holders, I decided, did not look at me but continued to leer at the adults at the ropes, who stared at the stylite, who glared at me standing in her line of sight. The adults were awaiting the next signal to haul at the boulder, so I took the arm of the nearest boy, the stylite threw her head forward and exhaled, and the adults drew themselves again into their exertions. The boy came with me and so long as he was not in direct view of the ropes served well enough at his task. I taught him his movements—left a little, backward, forward, and so on—and handed him a plumbline so he might learn what I meant by straight. During this extended period of productivity, as I triangulated from one contour to another away from the boulder, and then via a series of flying levels back to its datum mark, and although my other assistant talked in great detail about his former employer, I heard little of it. Only once we were sitting that night with our sticks, roasting the tubers, did I hear again what he had to say, which was still about the priest, and about what the priest had said, and so on. I am particularly intrigued, the priest told us, my assistant was recounting, by how you have made this second priestly figure shrink back from excessive stimuli. You introduced a degree of artificial dullness into your creation which I did not think of introducing into my own. I did not think of this when I made the first automaton, which is entirely understandable, he said, given how the first automaton was a less sensitive device and there was much less reason for me to consider doing what you did. Still, I am not sure I at all realised the significance of producing a machine which does not merely respond to stimuli, but seeks to protect itself, as it were, from any excitations that rise above a certain level of intensity. I think I knew this is what organisms must do, and this was how the first organisms most probably survived. They developed skin and placed a barrier between the outward excitations and their sensitive innards. But when I look at you, I am not sure that you have thought it through in these terms, the priest said as we listened. I can see no evidence that you have thought this through like I have, he went on, looking at the taxidermist most particularly. I suspect, he said, that you still fail to appreciate, as I failed to appreciate, but as I have now understood the significance of skin. You merely selected thicker skins because that is what you decided to do. You decided for thicker skins and so these were the skins you selected. Your decision and your action operated on the same plane so that your decision might as well have been your action and your action your decision. I have seen this often enough before with institutionalised types, the priest said, looking at the first apprentice now. I have noticed how these people think. Institutionalised people have given up the ability to decide, they merely act, he said, and yet, each action is already a decision and so hardly an action either. It is because they mistake actions for decisions that institutionalised people are still convinced they decide, and because they mistake decisions for actions they are still convinced that they act. The institutionalised have no idea their actions are already decided, he said, and they have no idea what an action without decision might look like, just as they no longer understand how to reach a decision, how to deliberate without acting. My assistant paused, I recall. We sat roasting the tubers and he paused for some time. I turned my tuber several cycles, inspected it again, and then again, and returned it hungrily to the fire once more before he resumed. I think I remember this rightly, my assistant said. I think I recall the logic as the priest told it to us, he went on. Certainly, I am sure of what followed. I am sure of what the priest said next, my assistant told me. There is no intelligence here, the priest said to us. I can detect no deliberation or thought even if what you did was actually quite something and might be assigned retrospectively, and falsely, as a stroke of genius. You did not appeal to some external rationale when you opted for thicker skins, the priest said. Your rationale was integrated within your unthinking chain of decision and action. It was nothing more than a turn for something more durable that reflected, in its logic, the irrepressible circularity, the durable stupidity, of institutionalised thinking. Whereas I always chose the thinnest skins, you chose ones that you thought would be more enduring. You decided your skins should be plush and turgid and fatted, whereas I was satisfied with skins that were only taut. Do not look at me as if you reckoned what you did, the priest said. I think we hardly looked any different, my assistant told me. But thinking we did look as though we reckoned that we knew, or saying that we did look that way even if we did not, the priest chose to repeat his claim against us. Despite your innovation, your achievement was a witless one, that is to say, you were witless creators. It is clear to me you still do not understand what I now reckon to be the magnitude of your discovery. By your decision or was it your action to opt for thicker skins, you prompted me to reflect upon the role of skin in the life of the organism. Without skin there would be no inner world. Let me explain what I mean, he went on. Without skin the outer world and the inner world would remain merged. Skin allows the inner world to exist within its own volatilities, affected by the outer world for sure, but not overrun by it. You merely constructed the second automaton with skins as you had seen the first automaton constructed. Skin to you was simply its coating, a camouflage, a cover for its mechanisms, and the simulation of my own outer layer. You took animal skins and stretched them over your admittedly more sensitive internal devices and when you stretched those skins you were primarily concerned with how they looked and not how they functioned. You said the skins of your priest machine needed to look a little more plumped, he said, eying the taxidermist again, I thought, as he said it. But when you did this, you mimicked more than the appearance of priestly skin. You reproduced the function of that skin. Without fully knowing the significance of what you were doing, you clothed your automaton with a layer of animal flesh which would serve to dull the sounds and the impacts of the external world. I think I understand now, he said, how organisms developed skin as the condition of their inwardness, and how they isolated themselves from one another as a consequence of that skin. They crawled under or took against the currents of their liquid environments, defining their wet innards as different, as separable, as places that would contain their own oceans and swells. This was how each existed within its own primitive outer layer, he said. As isolated units. This was both the poverty of life at that moment and the condition of its possibility. These organisms did not opt to share a membrane as they might have done, and surely this decision was decisive. It was a crucial step not to share a membrane or merge with the membrane of another and so grow by association to become an intimate, mutually fluid, barely separable assemblage of creatures, made of interpenetrating flows and excitations, perceptions intermingled, liquid tongues interlocked. The priest looked at us, I recall, my assistant said, to see if we might react at all to his eroticism. I suspect we remained impassive. I believe that when the priest paused with the words liquid tongues interlocked still resting as a trace on his own tongue and palate, we hardly moved at all. Each organism guarded itself within its own membrane, he went on. Instead of interpenetrating one another in a continuous, invasive embrace, they sequestered themselves. This was their primordial jealousy. If anyone wishes to trace the origins of jealousy, this was it, he said. These outer membranes managed the ingress and egress of energies for each sequestered organism just as they managed the ingress and egress of solids and minerals. You should know that the first complex organism had a mouth, he said, and that mouth functioned as its anus. The first true animal can be identified at this point, benefitting as it did from the existence of an orifice that was both mouth and anus, and which enunciated by disgorging and engorging, selectively opening but mostly shut, preferring to heave and retch and swallow down rather than unseal itself to external, and potentially overwhelming forces. It opened its mouth which was its anus only for as long as it needed to. And this you should picture, the priest said, my assistant told me, as I held the stick, roasting the tuber. These organisms were not gaping at the mouth as you sometimes gape at me but held themselves with their mouths tight shut so the barrier between their insides and the liquid outsides would be maintained. These were simpler times when simpler things understood themselves in their natures. If you ingested and excreted by way of the same orifice you would know what I mean. I would have nothing to tell you if you were organised in this way, he said, and you would understand yourselves in your natures too. You would already understand all this I tell you if your anus functioned as a mouth and if your mouth functioned as an anus. You would see how the mouth and the anus are tied together and basically have the same qualities. Each must be regulated in its opening and its closing, he said, and what each emits must be closely rationed. But I see you do not perceive their connection, even if I can see that connection in you, as you look at me, and as you open and close your mouths. And so you must listen to me closely, he said leaning in. Listen to me now and ensure you follow my advice. Make sure you give your automaton an anus. Give your creation an anus, he said, and then sew it up tight. Any animal will do but make sure the materials you use are adequate. It is absolutely essential, he told us, that all orifices are closed, particularly those lower down, and especially that orifice we consider our lowest, since the materials you use for the construction of your machine are given to putrefy, as you can already see, and they will leak downwards and out. This must be controlled he said. You cannot allow your machine to leak its waste upon the floor by bursting from any point, which it will if you do not plan ahead. If it shall leak, as it must, it should leak from that orifice. Its leakage must occur against a refusal to leak. That refusal, even as it fails, will produce its continence, or a simulacrum of continence, a functional, organisational tightness, which must become the fount of its inner pressures, these forces that are the materials of its consciousness. And so you must give it an outlet, he said again, and only open it to the full slew of its contents when you are ready with a bucket. You look surprised, the priest said looking at us. I did not think it likely, my assistant said looking at me, but this is what the priest told us. He would frequently tell us we looked surprised, or disgusted, or confused, but how we looked hardly changed, I thought. We continued to sit as we always sat, absorbing the details of his description and not digesting them overly much. We were not there to reflect, not to ruminate or even think. We stored everything he said for the purpose of application. We stored it all with only that in mind, studying the priest for the automaton—there was no space left to think with. Perhaps it surprises you to hear I have knowledge of such things, he continued. I should tell you that the lord inherited a library when he took this castle and I have been visiting that library for some time, first liberating it of its religious texts—these I fed to the skies—and then studying the remainder, holding the books open on those pages which mean something to me, and then leaving them that way across the various surfaces and recesses of my chamber until each book will not close nor will it open on a different page. There is a book with a passage on primordial creatures, the first creatures, it says, benefitted from their membrane, the first creatures, it is written, were dependent upon the inauguration of a barrier, were reliant upon surrounding themselves with a primitive skin, the word skin is written, and from this passage I have judged the story of their development, not as told in that book, I have not read the book, but the story of their development as it is implied in that passage. I have understood all this by extrapolation and interpolation too no doubt. I have extrapolated from the first creatures described in that passage to the first humans, and from the first humans to the last humans. I know as I look at you now that this first skin, this natural mechanism of self-defence, would later, much later, become the model of the human intellect, or the intellect as we know it. This first skin would later, much later, enable the intellect to take possession of itself, and become, at last, the specific intellect we call the human intellect, and which we covet so possessively, or so jealously, he added with a nod, even if there is so very little to be jealous about. The first membrane formed around the first and simplest organism anticipated the last thought you just had before I arrived at the workshop, the priest said, looking at the horologist now. It enabled the first organism to listen to its own excitations without so much exterior noise. It allowed that listening to develop into the activity of sending out and receiving minor impulses, again without overmuch interruption from outside. Only on the condition that the sounds and energies of the world were dulled could it develop its interior life. The first humans benefited from this dulling of the world just as much as the first animals did. The first humans profited as much if not more so, encased as they were within their thick skulls as well as their skins. But they lumbered about for centuries not knowing what to do with the wet, muffled darkness within their heads. It was left to our intellectual ancestors—those we associate with the birth of reason, the birth of art—to occupy these spaces and fulfil the destiny of skins. So trapped were they, so well insulated had they become, these intellects misperceived their inner reverberations for universals, and began to judge the world outside according to the pure isolation that the thickening of the skull promised but never entirely delivered. Their hominid cousins had thicker skulls, of course, the priest said, and so did most larger animals, and it is hard to decide why they were not similarly afflicted, if indeed they were not, for who is to say that a mammoth, or a hippopotamus, has not become lost within its own universals, whereas humans, we humans, are still buffeted in our consciousness by external forces and have not yet achieved the quiet retreat and grace of the megafauna. I have come to understand this process now, he said, by extrapolating in this way. I can see how this rejection of all intensities was taken up by our pagan ancestors, and then the priesthood, and then by the intelligentsia too, so that it became a mark of distinction and refinement to retreat ever further into all kinds of self-moderation and sensual privation which further enhanced the effects of the first skins. The skins you used, always from hides thicker than my own, I note, quite unthinkingly reproduced this conditioning effect of intellectual development. With the skin of brutes, you ensured that excessive touch, or sound, or light, would filter through and produce responses, but without over-animating your machine in doing so. With the outside world muted in this way, you allowed the automaton to draw direction from its cushioned and lightless insides. I can see how you engineered it despite yourselves to mimic the fundaments of intellect. As you stowed its mechanisms within its skins, you enabled its retreat from anything bold, or irregular, or overly enlivening, and as you did so you managed to simulate my inwardness. It is obvious to me now that when you observed me closely, just as you observe me here, you did not see me in the extent of my accomplishments and did not realise in that moment how to remake them. Everything you achieved was the result of mimicry and accident. And in a profound sense perhaps you are right, the priest said, and this is what my inwardness amounts to. It could well be, he admitted, that you have perfectly reproduced my seemingly profound, and to some extent unique, but nonetheless imitable condition of self-retreat, merely by placing sensitive mechanisms within the lord's offcuts. It seems you have quite unthinkingly reproduced the effect of my monastic training, its habituated withdrawal from the world. You have simulated the very conditions that define my priestly outlook. It appears you have replicated the originating fount of my priestly values, those values which teach that diminishing sensations are holy, which pacify the spirit when it threatens excess, and which cultivate religious ecstasies only insofar as they can be bridled. That inwardness which you imitate in this mechanised priest of yours took me years to cultivate but you conjured it again in a matter of weeks. There is no gentle way of saying this, he said, but I can see you made this priestly machine in the image of a resolute, shrinking idiocy, and that in doing so you made it as an imitation of what you saw, even if you did not realise what you did, even if you did not intend to insult me with your mouths again tightly shut—and I am not insulted, he added—even if everything you did you performed in good conscience, precisely this is what you achieved. If I understand you correctly, he added, with a glance, this is what you have done. I wonder, here, indeed, he went on, if you have successfully conjured my intellect as it lives in my own head too, he said, and not only my religious values, and my inwardness. I suspect you have, in effect, engineered the contours of my thinking from the gestures you observed. I have a fancy that on some level my intellect is today, at this very moment, doing its work within this creature that you have assembled largely from offcuts, from the lord's abattoir, and that my intellect now reigns to some extent on this workbench, that it has come to function in some way within every retreating gesture that your machine performs—since every gesture is a reproduction of a gesture you have observed, and every gesture you observed was a feature of my shrinking idiocy as you have figured it. And perhaps there is no other way to describe it, this condition which we have been told for centuries is not idiocy at all but its fierce opponent. We may have no option left but to reverse this judgement and identify idiocy in the highest intellectual accomplishments. I rather think, he said, that with every retreating impulse which this automaton has since produced by its own mechanisms, the machine has started to take its own initiative, and that in death it has started to reckon, and that your automaton has, at least to some extent, acquired its own thoughts. I suspect your creation has already begun to extend itself beyond its muse, and that it has started to travel to a region exceeding my own achievements. Your machine manages all this, he said, as it trades gestures with the world on its nodding donkey. It was at this point, my assistant said, that my mouth again opened, for I was informed as such by the priest. This is what the priest said, my assistant reported. Oh, look, your mouths have opened again. And I recall looking at the horologist, at the taxidermist, and at the first apprentice, and confirmed that each did have his mouth open, as I did too, he said. As I listened to my assistant go on with his recollections, distracted by the telling of his memories, speaking them with his meal burnt on the stick and mine still rotating, I wondered if the priest he recalled was in actual fact more likely pulling his leg.

When we first received instruction from the priest, my assistant said, the priest told us to look out for his transcendental gestures. He invited us to observe him very closely and take good note of anything he did, however minor it was or apparently incidental, anything at all which might have a transcendental air about it. This, he declared, is what you must repeat, because that is what lay behind the success of my first automaton. His first machine beguiled the peasantry only on the strength of its transcendental gestures, he assured us. I cannot recall exactly how I constructed them, the priest added, gesturing vaguely at the memory of what he had done—was this a transcendental gesture we wondered—but it was essential each gesture was produced in response to a chain of causes that lay outside the automaton itself. No gesture could be planned in advance. The automaton could not arrive at each dwelling and cycle through a list of grand movements designed to signify a divine lesson, a godly effect. It must produce its enormities in response to each situation, he said, and thereby establish a natural link between the quotidian world and the world of celestial intentions, never knowable in themselves and transmitted only by allusion. The automaton must allude, the priest said. It commands by its allusions just as I allude to you now. You must instil this art of suggestion, he told us. And suggestion, he said, is most effective if the one who makes the suggestion places the origins of suggestion in others, never himself. A priest never himself suggests, the priest said, but draws each suggestion from those or that which is alluded to. The art of suggestion, which is the art of religion, is to prey upon ideas already in motion before your arrival. These are the ideas that the automaton must amplify, just as I was taught to amplify doubt, or pain, or love, ruling the world of men by intensifying their experiences and then demanding they be enchained. I have seen market criers do much the same, the priest said, albeit more crudely, he admitted, as they watch men and women and children approach and manipulate their desires by proclaiming those desires at a greater volume, at amplitudes where desires are distorted into catastrophic demands—surely market criers have the end of the earth already resounding in their hoarseness, he added. Market criers are permitted to shout for the souls of others, to ventriloquise each soul's desire to shout for itself, and, I suspect, the priest went on, the day will come when their crying will approach the sophistication of today's priesthood. The day will arrive when market criers shall learn at last how to whisper as we do, but in whispering they will only shout more effectively, and amplify each soul they command through that whispering, because ours is still the more subtle means to make the souls of men swell and open themselves to manipulation. But that time has not yet come, the priest told us. The soul is still ours to manipulate by listening and by responding quietly to what we hear. For this reason you must build receiving devices, and these you must place across and within your second automaton to enact these causes and project them inside the machine where they will work its mechanisms. The horologist asked him what he meant precisely, and could we see the kind of mechanism he had in mind at work in the first automaton. If we could see exactly what he meant, we might model our efforts upon it. The priest responded with a different gesture, now one of dismissal, and told the horologist that the first automaton was by this point too far decayed and we should leave it in its corner. Actually, he went on, I would like you to draw the hood still further over its face. We are not to look at it, he said, and should let it alone. And so, our famous prototype remained like this, sat there, and functioned only as a rumour of its former efficacy as told to the lord by his informer. We did never see it in action, and the second automaton relied heavily on the ingenuity of the horologist, the taxidermist too—each brought their own interpretations to bear, hoping to enact whatever vague notions the priest would give us. He said each transcendental gesture must be an interpretation, and that what we were building was a master interpreter. Your mechanised priest must be sensitised to all manner of small sounds and human movements, and it should imitate them too, at times, with such clicks and groans and breath-making artifices as you can design. Imitation is indeed the first step in priestly interpretation, he said, because the priest must be seen to be listening, and must be seen to receive those very signs he will consider by repeating them in himself. I suggest we begin with a thin membrane, the taxidermist said, one resembling the ear drum. Several of these might be produced, arranged to reverberate at different frequencies. Yes, yes, very good the priest replied, not quite indicating if this was precisely what he had done with the first mechanised priest but not quite denying it either. Or coils of metal, the horologist ventured. We might employ a bimetallic strip which responds to the warmth of touch. Or a human hair connected to a device that would function like a mechanical hygrometer, he went on, with it responding to the moisture of breath, of speech and supplication. The horologist was overcome with enthusiasm at last. At this point I myself took the billows from the fireplace, said my assistant, and took the device to the priest and ventured—*and this in miniature could simulate priestly breathing could it not.* Yes, yes, all of that, the priest replied in his noncommittal way. But first of all, the automaton imitates. Priestly authority relies upon priestly imitations. The priest can only function by establishing a line of connection with the lives he administers, and if the priest is called most often to a suffering household, is most frequently brought into the household to respond to the demands made by suffering and to administer in turn his strategies and his lessons in suffering, then the priest must imitate this suffering too. Every priest must be an exemplary sufferer before all else. The pain of others must be manifested in the simulated pain of the priest. He must suffer in ways that are recognisable, if not also always a little removed. His authority relies upon that fact, upon having borne the same pain, having himself suffered a bodily constitution that is just as weakened. Priestly authority originates in his weakness, in his deep susceptibility to pain, which the priest has nonetheless suffered better, with greater virtue, and fortitude. For this is what qualifies him to interpret that pain in others and prescribe habits for living through its worsening. The priest does not offer salvation on earth but the assurance things will only get worse. They must learn to make a lesson of their suffering and build everything upon it, the priest said, my assistant told me. We will capture a peasant then, the first apprentice said. We will find a miserable peasant, the first apprentice declared. We will trap the worst example of human suffering and make sure our automaton repeats it. I suggest, he went on, that we keep the peasant caged here in our workshop and that we study every grimace he makes. I suggest you make a sketch of each contortion, the first apprentice told the taxidermist. Or a model. We should set an easel before the peasant, or perhaps we can model each grimace in clay. Doesn't every peasant grimace a little differently though, the taxidermist replied. Could one peasant ever represent the full range of facial distortion, he went on. And doesn't the priestly art reside in having witnessed that full range of pained reflexes. Would one peasant be enough, he continued. Would we not need to imprison a dozen, at least, and study them in all their variety, the taxidermist asked. The first apprentice replied that we should start with one, but that he had no objection to expanding our menagerie, as he called it, of human pain. The priest waved him away and with a creeping smile continued to talk. That smile lay ghosted on his face even as it was far diminished and overtaken with the movement of other words, my assistant told me.

When the priest next came down from his chambers and found a peasant in the workshop, shackled and groaning, he looked surprised, or looked like someone who had just been surprised, and asked us what it—the peasant—was doing here. After that the first apprentice brought no more peasants to study and poke at. We each returned to our own bench within the workshop and continued to refine our mechanisms.

The priest led us to understand that our efforts to reproduce his transcendental gestures were governed by a more immediate need. These gestures were not simply part of the automaton's arsenal, the priest explained. I have not told you, he told us, to reproduce my transcendental gestures merely so that they may do the work of ruling others as I once ruled them. The automaton needs to learn transcendental gestures for its own material survival. These gestures are necessary, he went on, because they help to simplify how the machine responds to the world. Simplification, he went on, is actually central to your work, he said, at which point the horologist and taxidermist looked at one another and then across at their workstations. You are great simplifiers, essentially that is what you are. Despite all your accomplishments, and I can see they are considerable, the two of you in particular, he said to the horologist and the taxidermist, are basically simplifiers. You consider your work complex and believe yourselves to be agents of complexity, but really all your work amounts to is the extended work of reduction. And now you must enable your automaton to simplify too, he said again once he had their attention. Like you, your machine must be governed by the law of simplification. Without that ability, it will destroy itself. If you do not equip it with my gestures, he went on, your automaton will seek to respond to every single movement it detects and thereby it will destroy itself. Even with its skin as thick as you have made it, your machine will attempt to react to each signal which does make its way through, and these signals will accumulate and become too much for it. I find it remarkable your machine has survived this long, he said. Just you mark my words, soon it will begin to fidget like one of the lower animals, as a rodent fidgets or an earwig on its back, but it lacks their supple nature, and so will destroy itself. You made this thing from the flesh of the larger animals, those which move slowly. Worse still, you made it from the flesh of domesticated animals. These animals cannot endure too much stimulation and their offcuts cannot endure it either. The remains of domesticated animals are in many ways the worst materials you could use even if they are the most appropriate for that very same reason. Your machine will attempt to reply to every signal, and so destroy itself. It will be led to its own self-annihilation by way of itself, he continued, and will become prematurely extinct without my transcendental gestures. If you do not wish it to self-destruct, you will do this. You will study me and have your automaton gesture to things beyond this world of immediate perception just as I gesture to them, he said. My gestures here are crucial, he told us. They are acts of interpretation which are always at the same time agents of simplification. By concentrating all the automaton's movements into reduced, and symbolic interpretations, it will do this too. So watch me, he told us, and see how I reduce my surroundings by gesturing at them, see how I survive myself by blinding myself to so much of the world I inhabit.

The peasant also told us something, my assistant said, I recall it now, he added. And he paused. And I listened. Do you know, my assistant said, looking at me oddly as he did so, I remember that thing the peasant told us before we released him. As my assistant remembered what the peasant told him, I began to wonder if he was fabricating. I came to suspect as I had not wondered before if my assistant might be an industrious fabricator, an incontinent storyteller, and if some if not the greater extent of what he told me was not recollection but invention. It came to me that his materials were not so much memories re-told with peculiar clarity but experiences of our time together that served to detonate reactions in his mind. These were used to inspire his telling, warped somehow by his innards into a malicious un-telling, or otherwise-telling of what he saw. If so, it was all of it mixed with memories and other tellings that he had been told but was not tied to them. He was incontinent either way, but this could change how I received his incontinence, I thought. Incontinent recollections are received differently to incontinent inventions. Each has its own evaluative realm, its own norms, and its own limits. In the world above, incontinent inventions are generally received better—I believe they are at times lauded—whereas incontinent recollections are more typically suffered under duress. But in this world below the evaluative order is upturned and incontinent recollections were easier to bear. They held less threat of messing with my understanding of our predicament. I remember it very well, he said again looking at me as he did so and then looking at the rift sky above us. I remember it and my memory is not mistaken. The peasant, he said, said something about a great cut, a rift in the earth. The peasant told us it was rumoured to lie at the borders of the lord's dominion. He told this to us as we peered at him to study his face and measure its contours, its crevices, and trace each line of pain. When the peasant told us this, his face was still at a grimace, and so we attended to him closely. The taxidermist sat with the modelling clay and scored every line he saw, returning to join us and check as we looked at that peasant and as we noticed how his face moved, looking as we did for each supplementary frown. This is how we were arranged as the peasant told us that, precisely this and what I now tell you, my assistant said. He said there was a rift but the lord did not wish to know of it. He said the lord was merely interested in his own dominion. He told us the lord wished to measure every stream, every field, every ditch, and that the lord even wanted to know the precise dimensions of every latrine, and every dwelling house too, as well as every sty and every stable. The peasant told us, my assistant told me, that the lord had sent for a man who could do such things, a man who was equipped to measure his dominion, a man who knew about lengths, and levels, and angles, a man who could triangulate and turn his figures into drawings, a man who would convey the lord's eye by way of those drawings into each recess and hole, and that he would employ this man to measure every inch. The lord said he would have the man sit in towers to survey his lands and perfect his drawings, and that he would have these towers built so high they would sway. The lord said he would enchain the populace for the duration of his measuring to prevent them from moving or building new things. This would not be allowed before the lord knew about all existing things and where they stood. The lord said he would inflate a balloon with hot air from the fires of his kitchen and suspend the man below that balloon with a pen in one hand and paper in the other to capture every part of his dominion from every angle, hanging with his pencil and his paper below that hissing and slowly deflating bladder. The priest did respond to this, I think, my assistant said. He said something, I recall that he did. I am sure the priest said something in response, since I recollect listening to what he said. I cannot remember what his words were, but I do recall that he grinned when he said it. The priest replied to what we told him of the lord's wishes, he reacted to what we had learned from the peasant, and as he did so, that grin of his was unmistakable.

Days later, thinking we had not sufficiently understood, the priest returned to his earlier point. As you make the machine more responsive, and to that extent, more real, there is a risk that you will over-sensitise it. There is a very good chance, he told us, that your automaton will be overburdened by its experience of sound, and touch, and heat. It will become a victim of its sophistication.

This much we had since discussed between us. The taxidermist was concerned that his stretched-over drums, the vibrating skins, would tear as they thrummed, and the horologist worried that his mechanisms would generate too much heat and contribute to the premature decay of the organic parts. And so each attended again, in his own way, to the question of durability, of procuring parts that would not wear out so fast. The taxidermist was mainly occupied with acquiring better lasting membranes for the drum-like receiving devices he manufactured. He said nothing much could be done about the other organic parts we used to save them from their natural rot. He said rot was unstoppable and we should factor it in, to which the first apprentice replied, yes, but what about the animal heads in the castle, to which the taxidermist said, well but these are not designed to move, or sweat, or glisten as the priest's living flesh. We already picked over the lord's abattoir for the freshest materials, preferably those still warm. For his part, the horologist decided to insulate his internal mechanisms with furs. We placed these furs inside the machine, and so within its skin. The furs helped to some extent. They gave the automaton a gentle internal pressure which buffered its skin and bulked its features without pushing too hard at any point. Furs were longer lasting than the fats we previously used to pack out the innards. These fats were wrapped in narrow parcels of thin leather and needed to be frequently replaced. The packing out of the mechanism posed its own problems too and for which we subsequently found a solution. All of the more delicate mechanical parts were protected from this internal pressure by using the ribcages of small animals, generally birds, which were light and strong for the purpose. We placed traps along the branch of a nearby tree and caught birds of all sizes and hence casements of all dimensions, still reserving chickens for the larger mechanisms—here we turned to our daily meal for materials—and a swan for the largest, trapped by the first apprentice and garrotted by way of a rope loop at the end of a very long stick. And yet, much as we laboured to maintain the automaton and repair its various pieces as they decayed, we knew it would be necessary to eventually relent before the rot and rebegin with a fresh machine. There will come a point, the taxidermist assured us, where the rot sets in to such an extent it begins to spread across all tissues and nothing more can be done to patch it up. It was inevitable that the automaton would submit to this final necrosis. But over-stimulation would quicken this process, the priest was right, and it would do so by over-stretching and over-heating. Of that, they were certain. And there was only so much we could do against it.

The priest came a third time to explain the connection between the functioning of our machine and the nature and function of priestly gestures. It was clear to him, as it was perhaps not yet clear to us, he said, that the potential working-life of the automaton would be hugely reduced if its transcendental gestures were not perfected. So much of this lesson applied to us as well, he said. When I make recommendations for your machine, I effectively give advice to the world—as if the world needed direction, which it doesn't, the priest added, and this is the first argument against any kind of speech, first of all my own, and after that against all derivatives. More or less directly we were led to understand his lesson applied to us, my assistant said, trailing off for some moments as if trapped within the depths of his recollection and its implications. I heard the priest say that without his transcendental gestures— or their secular equivalents—we would soon become fraught and deranged. Without this repeated enactment of the eternal realm, he said, we would grow frantic before the ebbing away of each moment. We could not sustain ourselves before the tremendous, unflagging annihilation of every event in our experience by the passing of time. To which we said, yes, yes, but still the priest went on, not sure, as he told us, if we really understood him.

Our lives would become unbearable, he said, if we faced the destruction of everything we see before us. If we could just perceive this endless motion of present things becoming past things we would lose any remaining sense we had. Real perception of that perpetual loss of ourselves, of everything we have done, all we have seen sliding into its abyss would involve sliding with it, the priest told us. Total perception of that loss would be just another means of staring into the abyss which stares us back in any case. It would obliterate the seer, indeed, as there would be no means left to secure any conception of that seeing self, nor notion of its permanence before the sensation of all existences constantly falling into that oblivion we have learned to call, soothingly, our past. We said again, yes, yes, and the priest wandered off muttering to himself.

The priest next came when the first apprentice, the horologist and the taxidermist were all fully engaged, with the first apprentice holding open the skin at one side of a cut in the side of the machine, the taxidermist holding the skin at the other side, and with the horologist reaching far inside to replace a cam wheel which had lost some teeth, or so he had thought when previously holding his ear to the side—around the region of the kidney—and listening intently to its turning. Human beings are without doubt victims of those very intellects we helped place within them, our priest said. By furnishing our congregations with the means to think we made them suffer better, which is to say, we made them suffer worse. By giving them the concept of a past and a future we made them weak. We enabled them to conceptualise the present as a ceaseless event involving destruction. The present can no longer be experienced in its unthinking immediacy, he said, once it is conceptualised as the eating up of futures and the churning out of pasts. The horologist was caught by the priest's arrival with his hand deep in, just touching the cam wheel, as I have told you my assistant said, and the first apprentice and the taxidermist were caught too, although they had loosened their grasp, somewhat, so that the skin threatened to snap back and hold tight around the horologist's upper arm. None of them, myself included, wanted to give the priest the impression we were not listening. And that was how they remained, caught in this pose, as the priest went on with his explaining.

We gave our brethren, our followers, these tools to think with, so they would develop a need for our vision of another world, one above and beyond their own passing existence. But here I must speak plainly, the priest said, if you are to understand me correctly, if you are to properly enact the workings of my priestly logic in this device of yours. It is important to realise, he told us, that the eternal realm we offer provides no consolation as I have said before. Our eternal realm offers no consolation at all, he said, just as our pagan fathers offered little consolation of their own. We are not in the business of providing consolation, even if we are often called out for that reason. I know well enough when I approach a suffering household, when I stoop at the door and look inside, what they expect or wish for is consolation. And I do not doubt they sometimes find it, he admitted, although they find it only because they expect to find it. They see a priest approaching, walking through the yard, and they already feel consoled. But I never encourage it, the priest told us. I do nothing to seed this expectation of theirs. If they feel consoled in my presence, it is nothing to do with me. Take your hand out and listen, he told the horologist, whose hand subsequently emerged. Once we, once they, equipped humankind with the faculties of anticipation and of regret, once we enabled them to develop the capacity of intellectual pain, we did not offer some kind of religious medicine in exchange. We did not take with one hand so as to give with the other. Our eternal realm does not offer any kind of security or comfort, or nothing that lasts, because that realm is beyond experience, and so is by definition unreachable. No, this is not what I offer at all, the priest said. Don't hold your hand limply like that, he told the horologist, wipe it clean and attend to me closely now.

When I make my transcendental gestures, he said, I offer gestures which help organise existence. There is nothing redemptive about them. I offer an entirely different form of support, the priest told us. Not consolations at all, but habits to live by. I give men habits to live with, I give them habits to think alongside and by way of. Animals survive the impressions made upon them by acquiring their own brute ways, he said. This is how they manage to exist in the world and make it predictable for themselves. Habitual routes to walk along, habitual places to drink, habitual roosts to shit down from to those places where other animals are forced to crawl. And so too humans acquire habits. The only difference between men and animals, he said, is that men require intellectual habits as well as bodily ones. My religion, he said, is perhaps nothing more than a highly developed, highly institutionalised, and deeply embedded agency for the instillation of intellectual and bodily habits. It just happens to be one of the most enduring. My religion is just another system for stripping existence of its great, rich, and bewildering complexity, he said again. Every civilization has one. This is what it means to be civilized, he said. The civilized are merely those who consent to the organisation of their habits—their habits of thinking, and their habits of living. The civilized may still develop their own localised proclivities, he said. I can see that you have acquired some in this workshop. But you brought so many habits here already, and you rely on so many others when you leave.

My religion conditions what we are able to perceive, he said, by having it reduced to the organised frameworks of supersensual thinking. My religion targets perception and then narrows it, the priest told us, so that we can survive what we see. And insofar as the intellect is the product of religious thinking, or at least transcendental thinking, he said, and I hold this to be true, he added, the intellect owes its existence to this initial move. The intellect was only first produced as a result of this diminishment of perception. The intellect could only be developed in man on the condition of this prior reduction to a kind of thinking life that would, on the whole, never have any consequences or escape its bounds. It needs to be said, he told us, and it needs to be repeated, that the intellect in all its creative and spiritual profusion is not a treasure-trove of possibility but a mechanism for dulling us to experience. Not strong enough to endure the world about us in its raw and disorganised state, we must resort to these transcendental gestures, he said again. We feel that we have no option but to consign ourselves to some kind of unchanging substrate, something beyond the reach of decay, because even decay itself is too vivid. Human decline, the wasting away of life, the gradual descent into dotage, is still too much, still too full of the variety, of the exuberance of matter, for us to view it face on. And so we are determined to employ shades, and filters, and screens, to cast dotage, even, in a gloomy light. Without these mechanisms, the last fires of life, the decaying embers glimpsed through the cracks of its skin would be too much, too vibrant.

The first apprentice and the taxidermist at last let go of the skin at the sides of the mechanism, which clamped shut around the arm of the horologist.

Oh, I remember now, my assistant suddenly declared. I remember what the priest said after we told him the lord wished to employ a man who would measure every part of his dominion. The priest told us that the map the lord imagined would wage war on its own futility, that the map he envisaged would become its own anti-map, and that it would be a far better thing to divert the man from the lord's employment. Nothing is worth measuring so closely, he said. It is better not to see the lord's dominion as I have seen it. It is better not to look where I have been. The priest said this to us with a distinct and definite gesture of his finger. He said such a man should expend his energies far better by diverting his attentions from the measurement of the earth's crust which is, after all, merely the victim of its people, to walking the cracks of its hot and suspect foundations. Do you mean its magma, the horologist asked. You could call it that, the priest replied with another wave of his finger. We suspected, I recall, my assistant said, that we had just witnessed another transcendental gesture.

After a sucking noise the horologist was free. There was a long pause during which the horologist walked a full circle, returned to the automaton, and with the assistance he was given previously by the first apprentice and the taxidermist, extended his hand back into its innards. He said that he could feel the cam wheel, and yes it was lacking teeth, he just needed to unlock it from its mechanism. By touch alone, and with the memory of its arrangement, the horologist managed to disengage the wheel and draw it out. At this point the priest resumed, so my assistant recalled, and the three of them were frozen again in the same posture, holding the skin back, and with his arm deep inside.

Every interpretation is also a promise, the priest went on to say, and every promise rides upon a calculation. We saw how readily they forgot, how their forgetfulness was the condition of their robustness, and so we developed a counter-faculty. We taught them the instillation of memory, that kind of memory which carries its own mass and force. The faculty we taught them to live with would have consequences, is what I am trying to say, the priest said. Get your arm out, he said again to the horologist. Why do you keep sticking your arm in when I have things to tell you, he asked. Come here, he said, dry your arm on my robe and be seated. And to the others he said to dry their fingers and be seated also. Now listen, he said.

When we taught them the faculty of memory, he went on, we made it so they would never again leave so much of themselves behind as they moved onward. We raised them from their animal life he said. With our assistance, they would acquire a growing chain of recollections to think and struggle with and compare themselves against and by which tethering they felt their movements with added weight. At last they saw their past with fear and sorrow. Listen now, he told us, because this is what we taught.

If they suffered as they did, it was because of their uniqueness. Their suffering became a sign of their uniqueness. It affirmed them in their differences, he said. They affirmed themselves now by suffering, by committing pain to memory, and then by suffering it all over a second time, or as many times as they remembered and chose to remember. They carried their past sufferings with them and revived those past sufferings alongside each new affliction. These suffering beings, the priest said, were rounded out because of their suffering. See a wood turner turn a bowl and you will have some notion of what I mean. Or a pig's bladder, he said. See a man strain to fill a pig's bladder with his lungs and you will see things as I do. When I spectate human beings, he said looking down at us, I see balls of pain rolling about on the floor, clutching fond memories only to heighten the experience, living like that in a state of abject recollection. These individuals took form and developed identities, as long, causal chains of pain wrapped over themselves. Each became an inflated bladder, fearing the next pinprick, arranging all reasons for the injustices of their predicament across those fragile borders until that border zone became cluttered, and eventually blocked out the sun. This is what gave them security in their uniqueness, he said. Every human lines its walls like this, wishing to become rigid, finding its individuality in that thickness. Soon they will line their skies as they line their thoughts, and they will fill their skies with minor suns, except these will fall to earth.

This was how they adopted the faculty of memory, the priest continued. They adopted it as they dragged it all forward and suffered its repercussions. They found themselves encased within the chain of causal things we had caused them to construct from chance events. These chains of causality were not exclusively our own, the priest admitted, we took our materials from their basic customs and traditions, in particular their most violent habits. We took their still unthinking suffering, their chaotic but self-inflicted rites of pain, lacking organisation, lacking predictability, and we reinterpreted them. We reorganised their habits, he said, we made them predictable. We introduced ideas of equivalence, of uniformity, of sameness, and we gave it all back to them like that. We gave everything they thought they already knew and returned it to them in the language of equivalence, of uniformity, and of sameness. We returned their customs, their nascent culture bleached of its former, anarchic, forgetful restlessness, and gave it back infused with the deliberate, instrumental perception of our own. We finally had them see one another in this light, he said, as miserably foreseeable beings. We taught them to remember themselves by the promises we made, by the futures we reckoned, by the logic of calculation we instilled. We taught them their histories by setting out a terrain within which they could expect to move, and which would remain behind them as they did so. They would calculate their prospects within this landscape we described, and when we first designed it, when we first pictured that future terrain for them to move within, we ensured it was full of pits and caves, concealed entrances and sudden falls. We found that the reintroduction of a degree of chaos, and chance, encouraged their attention.

And yet, the priest added, our own priestly concentration waned. The priests could not hold themselves to their task. At this his eyes met ours, my assistant said. We saw how he looked at us with obvious disgust. Why are you sitting at my feet, he said.

As we moved off the priest began to inspect the trim of his robe, scratching at the dirt of our work that was attached to it, flicking small particles across the floor.

If I remember rightly, my assistant said, the priest now spoke more to himself than he did to us. Or so it appeared. Or this, at least, was the effect he had in mind to give. He did still gesture after all.

The supervision of others is our crucifixion, one might say, the priest mused, from which we must allow ourselves respite. There were times when we failed to promise with sufficient attention. Our promises do sometimes lack specificity. It has to be admitted that our followers must often make do with the old promises which we take from our book, and that we deliver these promises to them without all that much adjustment to their situation. The same promises, the same calculations, year after year. Most of what goes by the name of religion if not the whole lot of it all operates by way of this mechanism, he said. It recycles the old narratives, barely freshening them up.

The manner in which we operate as a priesthood has always reminded me of how I used to fish when I was young and before I trained. I stood facing the sea when the tide was low, casting out, hauling back, and then throwing those fish I caught into a shallow rockpool behind me. This depression was only as deep as the fish were wide. They could not swim away but lay on their sides. The fish I caught made do with the shallow water, one eye to the sky, the other against the base of the pool, the rock, living on like that by animal habit and reflex. These fish waited until I finally turned from the sea, walked back over to the small pool, and despatched them.

The priest also said that he who promises last, promises best, which is another way of saying he who lies last, lies best.

And he added that lies are not lies if they are not artfully constructed as truths.

And that the best lies always happen to be the best truths.

Even better lies, he went on, are those that are perversely counter-factual. Counter-factual lies muddle the faculties into submission, the priest said.

There is no God and Mary was his mother, was one of his favourites.

My assistant—for some reason I would keep calling him that—did maintain my interest however much I resented his telling at first. The boy I had recruited raised my spirits with his obedience, and the more the boy obeyed me and became efficient at his task, the more I allowed myself to listen to my assistant and his extended narration. I came to fear, indeed, that I had already missed many details of his account when we first entered the valley, and that I had not listened as well as I might have done back then during my initial preoccupations to find the boulder and fulfil my contract. It had taken me this much time to acclimatise myself to the narrow possibilities at the lower reaches of the rift, where the sun was becoming a memory of its heat, and where a man who would otherwise bore his listener was at last welcomed for his speech. I found that his monologue served to lighten the gloom—or at least give it contours—and that it extended or distracted me from the diminished prospects before us. For so many days I had lived without a smoke—my tobacco pouch long emptied—and the diet of tubers had worked its way from my gut to colour what was left of my formerly acute land surveyor's perception. These tasks preoccupied me less and his speech found no more pleasures to interrupt. Little more was left of my assignment in any case—for what else is there to know of the boulder—and so I listened more closely to what he had to say. With the region about the boulder mapped out, I would find myself sitting with my notebook open ready to transcribe his speech. But his silences had become longer, I thought, and carried with them less of what I formerly experienced as the threat of resumption. I came to fear, indeed, that the time would soon be upon him when he had nothing more to say and would not speak again at all.

As my preoccupation with the boulder wanes, I see he is watching the rock as I had once done, but with greater determination and persistence. I suspect he views it differently though. The boulder is weighing upon him, that is clear, and I am sure when he talks, he is no longer fully riveted on his own speech. When we were out of its range, when the boulder was no longer in our line of sight, I had the strongest intuition he would rather face in the direction of the rock we could no longer see, than face away from it. I felt he was also at times listening for it too, although the boulder makes no sound, merely the ropes and the efforts to haul it which could be heard during the day when we were in its nearest vicinity. The boulder, I am sure, has still not moved despite the daily exertions and the clear and obvious exhaustion of the valley dwellers as they sit each night around the fire. They roast their tubers and then fall back for the night, their meal often only half eaten, or with the stick upon which it was roasting falling into the embers from their exhausted hands. The boy and I have successfully plotted the rut of the boulder which leads up the valley a considerable way before turning about and making back for the deeper parts of the rift beyond which it presently rests. It is impossible to estimate the duration of its journey and so properly judge the length of the exertions that must have been expended to bring the boulder to its current position, but it feels no exaggeration to conclude that the boulder had been in transit for a very long time indeed, and that civilizations have risen and fallen in the lands above during its travel. This leaves the question as to the age of the rift people, and whether they have taken upon themselves the hauling of the boulder from an earlier group, or if they haul with their ancestors before them, and their ancestors too, which would make the rut itself the oldest surviving document in recorded history and its longest sentence, extending back before recorded history itself, in all likelihood. Their speech certainly seems hardly developed, and perhaps demonstrates the time they have spent in this valley committed to this task. Their talk is entirely formed of blunt sounds and gasps not all that much different from the sound they produce when they haul at the rope, which is not speech, but the noise of natural exertion. Certainly, it makes sense to me why they have been slow to adjust to our presence in the rift. They have not particularly noticed us, although there have been some indications. The boy is an exception. He is now well-adjusted to my voice. But I feel that the rest of them are beginning to adjust to us as well. I sense that they have begun to modify their behaviours, as the stylite seemed to first suspect they might, or so I thought when I looked in her eyes.

The lord eventually desired his own reproduction, my assistant recalled. As the lord entered the workshop, he said he would not have it ride on a donkey. This was the first we heard of his desire. He came to tell us that we were to remake him, the lord, from animal flesh. But he did not begin there as one might expect, fixating instead on this detail about how the lord machine would ride. The lord came in through the workshop door with the words, *but not on a donkey*. We stood about the workshop, halted in our activities, and the lord said again more slowly now he knew he had our full attention, *but not on a donkey I tell you*. Not on a donkey, he repeated. Only halfwit prophets and idiot priests ride on donkeys he declared. Listen here, he said, I wish you to mount it on a manservant. If a donkey comes close, you must have it slaughtered. The thing will have two legs, and these will be those of the manservant, but the arms will be mine. Strap the man's arms, the lord told us, and give your machine lord's arms. When it points, it will point with the lord's finger. The legs of the servant will follow, I will see to that. I have plenty of servants for you to choose from, the lord said, tall, stout, whatever you require, now tell me how to begin sitting, and where to sit, so that you may produce my double. We abandoned the priest machine we had just been working on and gave the lord our full attention, inspecting him as he had seen us inspect the priest. No donkeys, he told us again, sitting down. I have seen how your priest rides. The lord sat in the exact same position as the priest did, and as we leant in we leant forward as we did to the priest to learn the lord's features. He looked at us as we inspected him closely for the first time, and the lord seemed satisfied by our interest. The priest was not there that day. By this point he hardly ever descended from his chamber, mostly ignoring our requests, or if he replied, the priest responded to whatever we had said with the declaration, *but you must know me by now*. These days the priest visited very occasionally, and only of his own accord. It took us time to adjust. There was a time when we called on him whenever we needed to study, and the priest obliged. We would climb the stairs and knock on his door and the priest would come down and sit in the light for us to model the next part of the machine on the wrinkle of his nose, or the shrug of a shoulder, or whatever we happened to be working on then. The priest would already be holding court as we descended and tell us what he felt at that moment we most needed to know. It turned out that much ground could be covered in the spiral stairwell and the priest was already well underway with his discourse by the time we emerged in the workshop. Yet he had by now long fallen silent. These days he said nothing. Or nearly nothing. The priest replied only with the words, but you must know me by now, or some variation of them. And he said them without emerging, sometimes through the door, and so we descended again to the workshop without the priest. It came as some surprise that when he did finally learn of lord's request, he laughed heartily at it, his eyes watering. The priest laughed with an expression we had not seen before, and so had not yet modelled. None of the five priest machines now in operation could water at the eyeballs as he just did. But I suspect this gesture was not intended for us to see.

The priest did sometimes talk at greater length after weeks of silence, and we lived in anticipation of it. We had been delivering food and taking away his chamber pot without seeing a glimpse of the priest, and then he emerged, freshly shaven, and freshly disappointed, so it seemed, with the man he saw in his mirror. This is what drove him to talk that day. The priest gave nothing of the more personal sort away. He did not tell us in any detail of his pain, or what some might call his feelings. But he did tell us that he knew at last he was obsolete. His obsolescence had grown steadily, but now it was absolute. We no longer had any need of him and should stop calling up to his chamber. No, you really have no need of me anymore, he told us. He said we could easily keep reproducing the effect of his ministry so long as we kept more than one machine in operation, reproducing each failed part using the other as its model. His approaching obsolescence was already clear with the first machine we made of him, but he said we convinced him, by observing him, that he was still controlling the strings, or should I say, sinews, of the device, and that when it went out in the world, it was still his doing, and his work. But now that we had several automatons in operation, each could become the other's muse, and if mistakes were made, this would be equivalent to his own ageing processes. The priest said he could already see that he was accumulating defects himself with the passage of time, defects a priest knows well enough how to instrumentalise. It happens to be the case, he said, that the older a priest becomes, and the more defective he is, the better that priest is received. Very young priests always struggle against that perception, and although they might be more acute in the advice they gave, even if they might have the benefits of a quicker wit and a more discerning intellect, these young priests were always beaten by their more aged and palpably more defective seniors. This fact had long amused him, he said, but now it was bearing out in a different kind of way with the priest machines. He found it galling to think that they would accumulate defects more quickly, and to better effect, than he. The first automaton we built, he said, was already a defective copy. We aged him even at that early point by way of its imperfections. I did not tell you at the time, he said to us, but I saw as you made it how defective it was, how you had aged me in producing it. You have never made me look younger, only ever older and more depleted. He felt that the flesh we used for the cheeks sagged a little more than his own, although he did not tell us this, he saw it clearly, and realised that in the vicinity of its cheeks at least, our automaton would be better received. He could not hope to rival the first automaton when it came to the gravity of those parts.

I have released the boy from his duties. Our work is now done and soon we must return to higher ground. I did consider keeping him, he does hold the pole very straight, but the boy's manner is still restricted by the extent of his experience, and I have no confidence he would survive well in the world above. I am not sure what I was expecting, but newly freed, the boy has not re-joined his young companions, and I notice too how they have become listless, less focused on the daily activity of watching the adults haul at the rope. Instead, he stands at the base of the boulder and tells those at the ropes, left a little, backward a bit, straighten it now, and so on, which are the words I taught him to hear and which he can now repeat. These words are of course blunted under the influence of his own manner of speaking, but they are unmistakable as commands, at least to my ears, and perhaps also to theirs. They are also louder than the stylite's breathy exhalations, and I believe it is all serving to disrupt her.

The lord also commanded us to not take any pig's flesh from a pisser named Johnson. These were his words. He told us to specifically ask about that when we visited the abattoir for parts. He said we must always enquire with unflagging diligence whether or not these parts were from Johnson's sties. Actually, when you arrive you must make that possibility impossible. You should appear ready with a command, the lord told us. The best way to arrive in all situations is to come with an order pre-prepared. Whenever I arrive, in any place, I issue an order. It is the only way to establish your authority, he said. You do this best by catching your audience off guard from the outset. And so, when you go to the abattoir, the first thing you must do is this. You will tell those working there that you will not have any pig's flesh from the sties of that pisser Johnson. I do not want my double to be made of those parts. He did not trust this Johnson, he said, about whom he had heard certain rumours regarding what was fed to the animals. The lord had good reason to suspect, he said, what this Johnson character gave them to eat, and that what he gave them to eat was not good eating. He was also highly suspicious of how Johnson fondled his animals. Johnson is an animal fondler, he said. I will not have skin on my double's face that has been fondled by this Johnson character. This Johnson also happens to be an inveterate liar, he said, but was popular nonetheless in his part of the town, most probably because he gave free offcuts to the taverns. We retired to the nearby tavern each day after our labours in the workshop and had indeed eaten some of these offcuts. They came to us at our table dried and curled up, layered with salt. Are these Johnson offcuts, we asked next time we were in. The landlady nodded. We looked at those offcuts just presented to us, all dried and curled up as usual, and imagined Johnson fondling them. We also wondered what Johnson fed his beasts and noted between ourselves how Johnson had no more family members left. Yes, a tragedy, she said overhearing. Very sad, she added. So very sad, she went on. But Johnson now gets his warmth from the hogs.

Some days later, after we had long eaten and digested the offcuts—the landlady did not leave us until we did—we overheard a group at the bar gathered around their own bowl of dried hog. They were talking about Johnson, about how this Johnson lived with his hogs, and how he ruled over them, and cared for them, and slaughtered them. They said that Johnson referred to himself as their lord, and that he only fed his hogs if they snorted three syllables which sounded like, *his lordship*. Johnson was sure that when they snorted like this his hogs addressed him as his lordship, that they had learned to snort the words *his lordship* under his command, and that they revered him as he lived among them. The group at the bar seemed very pleased to discuss this as they chewed. They in turn toasted his lordship, fondly, I thought, and then one among them attempted to snort the words, *his lordship*, as the others bent over and clutched their bellies. Hearing them at the bar, it seemed more likely, we came to think, that this was the rumour which the lord objected to, and that he would not have his double made of another lord's beasts.

The lord came and went, my assistant said. He did indeed always come with a command, but soon we got used to it and were no longer surprised.

During the lord's absences between sittings the first apprentice was propelled from his settled condition of petty exactions to a more febrile command over us. Feeling the proximity of what he identified, wrongly, as the highest power, the first apprentice seemed to vibrate and very nearly come undone with his excitement. Or this was how the priest described it when I next saw him outside his chamber. The priest said that true power, and true nobility, comes from the ability to expend oneself without enslavement to any idea, least of all enslavement to misplaced notions of power, and that the first apprentice—of whom he had made careful study himself and had recruited to this position for that purpose—did not have the first inkling. The lord for his part had no idea either how to fulfil his command. The priest said it was entirely predictable, though not without interest, to see how the first apprentice responded to the lord's presence, given that he had no conception of power as an active, self-engendering force. The first apprentice only understood the lord's own logic of power—which was a logic of self-enslavement, a logic of non-power— by submitting himself to it, by becoming its slave, whilst thinking all the while, just as the lord thought, that he was reaching the height of dominion.

The priest said it was truly wonderful to see how the lord proclaimed his ignorance by demanding the making of his double. This really struck him, the priest told us, as a supreme moment in the lord's idiocy, the crowning moment, the most delicious example by which our ruler demonstrated his own petty enslavement. The lord has finally shown us all that he will never exceed himself, said the priest, because he can only see his future as self-imitation. The first apprentice has also given me pleasure to observe, but far less so, the priest said. The first apprentice is enslaved to the idea of a command structure, the priest said, and this is perfectly common. But the lord is enslaved to his own image, which is rarer, or if not rare as a concept, rare in terms of the prodigious levels of self-binding that the lord rose to. The lord has an image of himself, the priest told me, and that image rules him. It is truly marvellous to witness, he went on. The lord, said he, is too jealous of the world, and jealous of himself, to discharge himself with the full force and possibility of the resources he enjoys and control over which he somehow maintains. The lord is tied to himself, the priest said, and even when he attempts to act rashly, to give a command without sanction, to escape custom and law by demanding something completely irregular and without justification—and so finally expend himself as a truly unshackled embodiment of sovereign force—his demands can always be traced back to his psychological or morphological afflictions. Inspected closely, the priest said, my apprentice told me, the lord is nothing greater than the rumbling of his gut or a temporary blockage of his synapses. More typically, however, the lord acts with caution, a kind of fussy carefulness that is easily missed beneath his bilious and blustering exterior. The priest said that the lord did not have what it takes to expend himself, to achieve that higher nobility, that greater sovereignty he seemed to model himself on, and that by contrast he, the priest, at least understood his own capabilities, and this understanding better enabled him to refine his intelligence, and his cunning, which were the two major devices of his own, lower, but insidiously effective power over the world of men. The priest's own power, he said, was of a more systematic, manipulative, tradition-building sort. For the most part it operated by not openly declaring itself. It functioned by shaping the materials that served to condition outlooks, and so not in driving others by the nose, which was how the lord operated. It was too subtle for the lord, and therein lay its success, said he.

One of the chief evidences of the lord's poor grasp of the image he laboured under—the image of a great, untouchable commander—was his compulsion to self-preservation, his caution, his desire to retain the ability to command which was always greater than his desire to exercise it—which was not inconsiderable itself. The lord was a capricious executioner, one might say, or wished to appear that way, but would only ever target those who were already unpopular with others. This was how Johnson survived as long as he did, although even Johnson would at last be despatched, the priest predicted, when he too fell from favour with his local populace, from some offcut, perhaps, that Johnson had given them for nothing, but which was found to be infected with worms. When the lord demanded that he would not be mounted on a donkey, that his double could only ride on a manservant, he probably considered this a further example of his dominion over men, but really, this was just another example of his dependence upon them. I can see that you chose a servant with the widest neck, the priest observed, because nothing less would do to carry the weight of the artifice, but this too shows how he was mistaken, where the true noble must carry himself lightly, not hold himself so close to the ground and weigh himself so heavily with meats. The lord should have told you to build your machine lightweight, not envisage it in terms of its mass, and think already which servant would be strong enough to bear him. This lord views everything he sees, and everything he owns, in terms of its usefulness and in terms of its strength. And here most of all the lord reveals himself to be ruled by a flat, calculative conception of his own existence. We taught him to think like that, of course, the priest said, and to this extent he remains an object of the priesthood and the world it enabled him to perceive. Still, it is almost painful to see how catastrophically effective we have been in reducing the scope of human possibility. As the priest talked, my assistant said, he stood with the lord's double behind him. The lord's double sat in its chair, in the reclining seat we used when constructing and reconstructing these devices, and the lord machine looked at us with its green eyes and gesticulated with the contours of its face, stimulated into action by the sound we made. The priest did not wish to see it and always stood like that with his back to the lord machine. When it was mounted on the manservant, the priest left for his chamber and locked its door so that the lord machine could not approach him as it would approach others, shuffling towards them with its blind feet, commanding their stillness and their obedience. Unlike the priestly automatons which governed by their silences and drew all those in their presence to peel themselves back and turn themselves inside out to fill that void, the lord machine governed by the sound of its breathing and its groaning, these augmented by the sounds of the exertion of its carrier. Its noises erased all thought of escape and brought those present into the stupor of their command.

In the lord's presence we experienced relief, a relaxation of our mental faculties which the priest never allowed us due to the demands of his inwardness and how that inwardness acted upon us. Our mechanisms were refined by now, and the lord was altogether simpler and required far less attention to reproduce. We knew the fact of his simplicity already ourselves and did not need the priest to tell us so. The horologist seemed altogether more settled, and the taxidermist began humming again to the percussion of his cutting tools. When the priest visited, very rarely now, he told us that if we worked much longer on the lord machine our minds would atrophy, that we would develop a dislike of thinking, or at least of the kind of thought which observing him had once required, and that our dislike of thinking would eventually be transformed into our incapacity to think at all. Soon you will stop thinking, he said, and when that happens you will not notice but will think yourselves to be thinking still. The longer you attend to the lord machine, he said, the less you will think. The lord machine does you no good, he told us, because the lord is an undemanding sitter. When the lord sits in this chair first intended for me, when the lord sits here and has you observe him, his features are unexacting, and he has nothing of substance to instruct you. He lacks depth or the appearance of depth, the priest said. He does not push you as I once did to reproduce my complex skin, my facial gestures, my transcendental gestures, to wonder at the limits of perception, to question yourselves and your ability to make animal flesh radiate like my flesh with the force of its higher being. This lord machine may rely on the techniques you developed when you observed me, you may stretch skin in the same way and make it tremble and flex with the same mechanical devices, but your work has become uninspired and the automaton you have produced will only ever create secondary effects. These are all secondary effects, the priest told us with an expansive gesture which took in the entire workshop. You have each become secondary effects, said the priest, pointing to us each individually. The priest told us that he did not doubt the sophistication of our workshop. He said that we had attained skills only ever dreamt of before, that we were closer than any had ever been to reproducing the effect of the mask of the living man. But our work, the priest told us, had finally become predictable in its intricacies, in all its considerable subtleties. You, he said, pointing to each of us again, have become predictable with your techniques and your devices. And for this reason we were no longer able to study, he told us, even less appreciate and be affected by the world around us. The world we saw no longer troubled us as it once did, as the priest had once seen, so he told us, as he had once troubled us when he sat with us and gave us instruction. It made you vulnerable, said he, to experience the world as I taught it to you, and this enabled you to exceed yourselves. But now you have become settled in your accomplishments. You have retreated back into the organised mechanics of human living. There is nothing left for you to think, because nothing will stimulate you to further achievements as I once did and you are incapable of stimulating yourselves. We had stagnated, he told us. Our intellects had become sick with the immediate demands of our employment. We had become at last, and in every respect, the lord's employees. Our capacity to think, he said, was not destroyed by the simplicity of the lord. Perhaps he should clarify this point. The lord did not bring us down to the level of his own abject stupidity as we came to spend so much time with him, staring intently at his simple movements, at his ordinary reflexes. The lord was, indeed, a very predictable creature, but he was not without interest. If we had the ability to revel in his simplicity we would have seen that, said the priest. Even the lord might have stimulated us yet, he said, if only we had the capacity to make an enigma of his stupidity, to become repelled by the lord, and by that repulsion receive our own propulsion into fresh acts of creation. No, it was not the lord. We could not blame the lord for what we had after all done to ourselves. It was not his simplicity but our own inability to dine in it. Your capacity to think was finally destroyed by your sophistication, he said, which became a settled state. Your capacity to create was ruined by your attainments which seemed to you to be a sign of your completeness. You at last yielded to it. You have become enslaved to it. You have become its victims, claimed by mechanics, by your computations, you have become simplified again, but unlike the lord, your simplicity arrived as you yielded to complexity, as you gave in to the logic of calculation and organised thinking. Do not misunderstand me, he said. The achievements of your workshop are considerable—you are still remaking the human machine, gesture by gesture, and you still peer across its surfaces with considerable acuity. Nobody knew the reflexes of that mask better than we did. But this great proliferation of devices was killing our capacity to perceive, he said. It was the very accomplishment of the thinking mechanism of our workshop, of our workshop itself working as both a thought machine, and a thought annihilation machine, which had killed our capacity to speculate beyond that mechanism and see anything new about us. You have become insects to me, said he. You are ants now, the priest told us, and you will not even see me approach when I come to trample your nest.

When the priest left us and was gone we made our own pleasures. Arranging two chairs, we had a mechanised priest sit facing the mechanised lord, and to give each a start, clicked a finger between them. Retreating back and remaining very silent ourselves, we saw the lord machine respond first with a tick of its own, to which the priest machine then reacted after a meaningful pause, and so it built between them, these mutual stimulations rising to the full range of their gestures. We saw very well how famously the priest and the lord got on, how productively they worked together. They were inter-animated, and nothing would stop them in their reactive enthusiasm until the skin became cracked—such was their mutual arousal—and we were forced to wind them down.

Before leaving I decided we would follow the rut further than my initial survey of its first loop, and that we would cease to measure and plot its course and consent merely to climb into it and walk along it. We had with us enough water for several days, and to this we added some tubers we had already cooked and softened in the fire. These filled the bag I normally used to carry the theodolite, now abandoned on its tripod somewhere, I cannot remember where exactly, further up the rift. The lens was cracked, and the bubble level had been smashed, by whom I could not be sure, though I suspected the stylite, and would have been sure of it if I had ever seen her off the rock. It was possible she crept down at night, but I had checked before, and always found her in the same position on her haunches.

We have been in the rut for days. We soon reached its highest point and then followed it as it returned and descended back down the rift, as it went beyond the boulder and into its narrow twilight. Each day can be measured by the waning light, the strip of sky above us no longer blue, or black, but grey like the dust of the earth we now tread through. There is no moisture here anymore and nothing falls from above without colliding with the sides of the rift and gaining lodging there. We are far below sea level, but I cannot estimate how far. He still walks with me, but I suspect he would rather return to the boulder. I tell him they are hauling it in our direction, that all their efforts are expended to return the boulder to the depths of the rift. He does not talk. He ceased talking when we left the boulder. I have some pages still of shorthand which I transcribe to keep myself busy within this record of his recollections.

Even the lord's pleasures were doubtful, if not entirely fabricated, the priest said, my assistant told me. He would always wonder how he might profit by them, or what it would cost him, so that the one single man in that part of the world with the greatest means at his disposal was least able to enjoy them, the priest said. The lord machine was accordingly produced without any kind of levity at all about it, and we hung a weight within its throat to simulate that burden. With the priest machines it was always different. The priest never failed to regard us with amusement, or something like it when we studied him most closely, and this undoubtedly influenced our work, as my assistant told me before we departed for the deeper parts of the rift.

There was lightness in the priest's seriousness but only heaviness in the lord. He said that too before we departed.

As we walked onward through the rift, I wondered what the priest's lightness felt like, and how it could possibly be simulated with dead materials. I suspect the priest would have replied—far more easily than with living ones.

The rift is warming as we travel further into the crust and the rut is undiminished.

The priest said that the heaviness of the human soul is just another effect of the burden of being made to carry one. He said that the soul is so well massed by its contents, which are its encasements, and is made this way so it begins to crush in on itself, and that by crushing inwards the collapsing soul brings the rest of the body to feel its presence as a kind of wet suction or a fibrous singularity. Really, he had no words to describe it, but anyone who carries one will know. He said anyone with ears would hear that crushing sound as an argument against the burden of incarnation, as humans at least, and not as another reason to look inward for its supposed defects, so the soul might be submitted to interior cleansing. Nor would they cast a sly glance outward, looking for others to blame, leaving the soul itself, or the very idea of the soul, permanently unmolested.

He is still walking behind me; I can hear it. When we pause, he rests a few feet away.

I can hardly see well enough to write and suspect my handwriting is overgrowing itself.

Yesterday we returned. Emaciated.

I told him as we followed the rut that his boulder had clearly emerged from the asthenosphere and was now returning to it. I said it was on its way, but that we could easily beat it there. He told me it is time we left our journey inward and turned about. I did not realise until days later that this was the first time my assistant had addressed me directly without encasing his words in his narrative.

As we rest, I pass him each morsel by shuffling over to where he sits—we are now eating the last of our rations in flakes—and he says nothing, but I can hear him eat it.

I can now see, my handwriting did outgrow itself in the darkness of the rut and will require its own transcribing. As I wrote, his recommendation, his advice, that it is time we retreat, is now old, just a memory of speech, but I suspect he might be right.

It is hot and dark. The rut is undiminished. I think that I have found tools in the rut, ancient shards of stone beaten from an edge, but I cannot see them well enough to decide. It is worth asking what they might be used to cut against down here, where nothing grows, or appears to move.

There is almost no light left to navigate by, and I am writing largely with the memory of where my imprints must be on the page. To be sure I use a new page for each line. The rut is remaining and easy to follow. Undiminished still. And still. Nothing yet different. He was right to say that. Is he still there—yes. He is still here. Yes, again. Enough now. We are retreating.

I ate the last flake, silently, so he could not hear me doing it.

The activity at the boulder is changed. Nothing is as it was when we left it. The ropes lie flat in the mud and the Egyptian screws are inoperable—the silt within the pit has solidified about them. The stylite lies dead upon the boulder, or she lies motionless.

He told me that he, the second apprentice, was eventually dismissed by the first apprentice, who felt emboldened by the presence of the lord machine. I have no reason to doubt it.

He told me that the first apprentice was soon after dismissed by the lord machine. I have no reason to doubt that either.

I now suspect their language is composed entirely of words used to refer to the boulder, and that all the words they use are boulder adjectives, boulder verbs. This would be why they have ceased speaking. Their blunt cacophony and manner of interaction has lost its referent.

They hold rods, irregular, but unmistakable, marked with lines carved at intervals along them. Others haul minor rocks with offcuts of rope, walking in circles and loops that overlap each other. These lines and curves resemble the paths of charged particles in what will one day be called a cloud chamber. They seem to imitate the lines along the boulder, but then stray beyond those hieroglyphic imprints to form a profusion of overlapping lines and footprints and about turns, their former journeys trodden into each other and more or less completely over-written.

My assistant now sits on the boulder by the stylite, and I know it is time to leave them together, in company.

The priest said the nodding donkeys were not an insult but expressed the work of two thousand years of spiritual evolution.

He said their blindness was flatly paternal and that their emptiness perfectly reflected the situation of a defeated humanity—in these parts, at least. He said that in those regions power no longer required its former subtleties. He said people had now travelled to the bottom of themselves and had flattened out.

He told me I would flatten out too, and I realised, as he said so, that this was the second time my assistant addressed me directly without the weight of his narrative, or the second time I noticed it, which occurred before the first.

I fear he might be right.

And besides, he or that part of him that found itself within the outlook of the land surveyor was now tired of the rift, was done with the rift valley dwellers, had grown over the valley rim to wish for some other landscape. There would be scarcely a hill, not even a barrow. It lacked contours and was nearly white.

The priest would have said something about that, if only he could muster it.

It was probably time to retreat up to the first speaker, he thought, and then the one before that.

Wrap the thing in its vellum.

Or vellum-like material.

And with a smoke on his own behalf—a delicious, pointless intermission at last—announce the end of its telling.

Also available from SCHISM²

Tractacus – Róbert Gál
Subconscious Colossus – Carlos Lara
Slow Hot – Andy Choi
Snuff Memories – David Roden
An Ideal For Living – Eugene Thacker
The Autobiography of Leisure – Narco Pastel
The House of the Tree of Sores – Paul Cunningham
Left Hand – Paul Curran
Coma Crossing: Collected Poems – Roger Gilbert-Lecomte, translated by David Ball
A Slow Boiling Beach – Rauan Klassnik
Serial Kitsch – Gary J. Shipley
Sacer – Nicola Masciandaro
Amygdalatropolis – B. R. Yeager
All the Messiahs – Anonymous
Thank You, Steel China – Sean Kilpatrick
Crypt(o)spasm – Gary J. Shipley
O Gory Baby – Brad Liening
Squeal for Joy – David F. Hoenigman
Pussy Guerilla Face Banana Fuck Nut – RC Miller
Spooky Plan – Drew Kalbach
Vital Signs – Tyson Bley
Mask With Sausage – RC Miller
Death Salad – Brad Liening
Drive-Thru Zoo – Tyson Bley
Necrology – Gary J. Shipley & Kenji Siratori

Available from
SCHISM NEURONICS

Batesian Prey of the American Southwest - Sasha Hawkins
Pool Party Trap Loop – Ben Segal
Mineral Planet – James Pate
Interrogating the Eye – M. Forajter
The Selected Poems of Charles Tomás – Carlos Lara and Tamas Panitz
Book of Losses – Joseph Turrent
KRV – Oli Johns
Sourcerer – Jace Brittain
Sonnet Cycle – Tom Will
Burton's Anatomy – Ansgar Allen
Fall Garment – Paul Cunningham
The Isotope of I – Connor Fisher
The Reading Room – Ansgar Allen
You Alive Home Yet? – Daniel Beauregard
The Reaches – Ansgar Allen
> Get Back to Work – Jim Redmond
Everjescence – Tyson Bley
Work is Hard Vore – Philip Sorenson
Vagabond   Joshua Martin
The –Tempered Mid·Riff – Brad Baumgartner
I Get Groceries – RC Miller
Lynx Perpetual Lynx – Colin Post
Wretch – Ansgar Allen
A Large Retailer – RC Miller
Spelunker – Mike Corrao
Gynophobia – Tyson Bley
Normal Service Will Resume Shortly – Tyson Bley
Cyclops – Tyson Bley
Demon Drawings – RC Miller
Dark Poems – Tyson Bley
Frankencop – Tyson Bley
Celestial Chimp – Tyson Bley

Also available from SCHISM PRESS

And They Were Two In One And One In Two

Edited by Nicola Masciandaro and Eugene Thacker.

A collection of essays on beheading and cinema, with full colour interior. Contents: Dominic Pettman, "What Came First, the Chicken or the Head?" / Eugene Thacker, "Thing and No-Thing" / Alexi Kukuljevic, "Suicide by Decapitation" / Alexander Galloway, "The Painted Peacock" / Evan Calder Williams, "Recapitation" / Nicola Masciandaro, "Decapitating Cinema" / Ed Keller, "Corpus Atomicus" / Gary J. Shipley, "Remote Viewing" / Photography by Leighton Pierce.

Sufficient Unto the Day:
Sermones Contra Solicitudinem

By Nicola Masciandaro.

Bound by desire to refuse worry, to reject and throw it away the only way possible, by means that are themselves free from worry. If this is impossible – all the more reason to do so. I. The Sweetness (of the Law) II. Nunc Dimittis: Getting Anagogic III. Half Dead: Parsing Cecilia IV. Wormsign V. Gourmandized in the Abattoir of Openness VI. Grave Levitation: Being Scholarly VII. Labor, Language, Laughter: Aesop and the Apophatic Human VIII. This is Paradise: The Heresy of the Present IX. Becoming Spice: Commentary as Geophilosophy X. Amor Fati: A Prosthetic Gloss XI. Following the Sigh.

True Detection

Edited by Edia Connole, Paul J. Ennis, and Nicola Masciandaro.

The most intelligent series in TV history has opened strange crypts for explorers. This excellent essay collection reveals just how far the dark tunnels lead. Let it coax you from the comforts of death and fear, into detection of the guttering nightmare that is life, coldly seen. **Nick Land**

These essays reveal knowledge becoming an enigma to itself, revealing the brilliant futility of the epistemological project. **Eugene Thacker**

The Spectacle of the Void

By David Peak

The world has been swallowed by strangeness. A new reality – a "horror reality" – has taken hold. David Peak's *The Spectacle of the Void* examines the boundaries of the irreal and the beyond, exploring horror's singular ability to communicate the unknown through language and image. It is also a speculative work that gazes unflinchingly at the inevitable extinction of mankind, questioning whether or not the burden of our knowing we will someday cease to exist is a burden after all, or rather the very notion that will set us free.

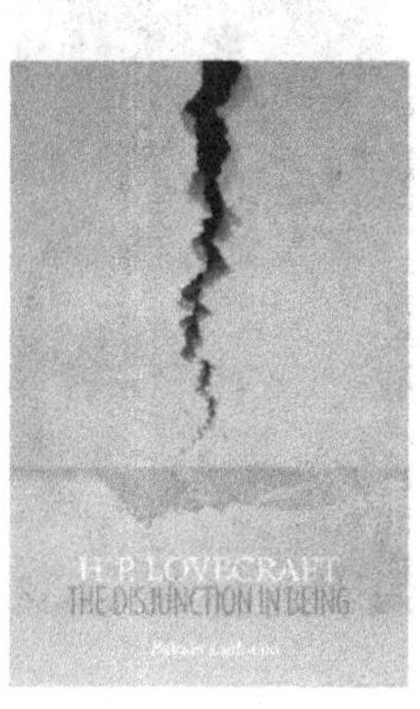

H.P. Lovecraft: The Disjunction in Being

By Fabián Ludueña

Lovecraft is "the most brilliant mythographer of the twentieth century." Rereading his oeuvre, philosophy will learn that true myth is the opposite of history, since it is summoned to enumerate the natural powers of the cosmos. At the same time, philosophy will learn that myth cannot glorify portentuous divinities since it reveals a transfinite universe become multiverse. In this key work of contemporary philosophy, the author shows that thought is not born of wonder but of horror: humanity's assumption of its non-place in the world. **Emanuele Coccia**

Mors Mystica

Edited by Edia Connole & Nicola Masciandaro

Contributors: Drew Daniel, Brad Baumgartner, James Harris, Teresa Gillespie, Charlie Blake, Daniel Colucciello Barber, Caoimhe Doyle & Katherine Foyle, Gary J. Shipley, Heather Masciandaro, Simon Critchley, Dominik Irtenkauf, Brooker Buckingham, Hunter Hunt-Hendrix, Niall Scott, Jeremy Dyer, Eugene Thacker, Dylan Trigg, Edia Connole, Nicola Masciandaro, symposium photographs by Öykü Tekten.

Serial Killing: A Philosophical Anthology

Edited by Edia Connole & Gary J. Shipley

Those screams you're hearing are philosophy being awoken from its dogmatic slumbers with a stark brutality rarely matched in the history of intellectual anomaly. If there's a more intense sleep-killer compilation out there somewhere, it's concealing itself well. **Nick Land**

One of the deepest and darkest truths in psychoanalysis is about the serial nature of the object. We pretend that it is unique, irreplaceable, singular, but it isn't. In this fascinating collection of essays edited by Edia Connole and Gary Shipley we find out about this serial perversion of everyday life. **Jamieson Webster**

The Isle of Lazaretto: Studies in Separation

By Márk Horváth & Ádám Lovász

Books are there to amaze us: Márk Horváth and Ádám Lovász have certainly done that. I'm not sure I've read a more paranoiacally invigorating and inclusive text since Negarestani's *Cyclonopedia*. This book is a wonderful mashup of critique and mysticism, deconstruction and speculative realism. It's like *Dialectic of Enlightenment* on bad acid and crammed with scientific research. The reach of scholarship in here amazes me: we've got OOO and Deleuze, but we also have Lyotard and Irigaray and Blanchot. This book is an invaluable polemic against the idea that breaking down the boundaries between things is always best. **Timothy Morton**

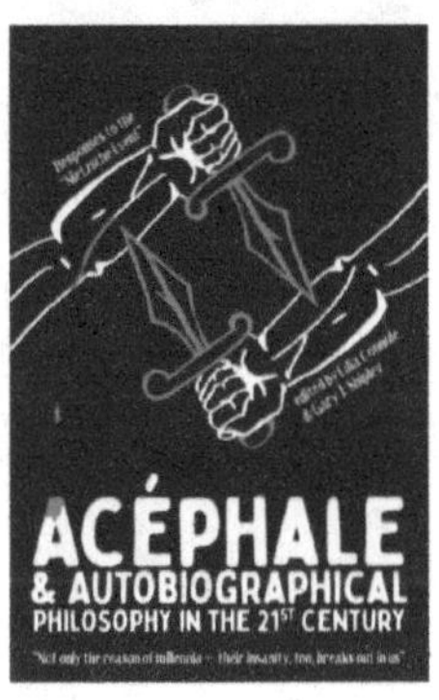

Acéphale and Autobiographical Philosophy in the 21st Century

Edited by Edia Connole and Gary J. Shipley

The volume is both erudite and visceral, it comprises historical and biographical knowledge, illuminating the Acéphale conjuncture through research and interpretative, intertextual connectivities, and it is raw, it lives with its material; it asks us to both respect and transgress the orthodox modes of "scholarly" endeavour, to see both as complementary and necessary, in alignment with Bataille's proposition that: "We need the system and the excess." It suggests answers, without solutions, to the questions: how to write, and think acephalically? **Patrick ffrench**

SCHISM²